VOYAGES

VOYAGES

A novel by
DORIS BUCHANAN SMITH

Viking

VIKING
Published by the Penguin Group
Viking Penguin, a division of Penguin Books USA Inc.,
40 West 23rd Street, New York, New York 10010, U.S.A.
Penguin Books Ltd, 27 Wrights Lane, London W8 5TZ, England
Penguin Books Australia Ltd, Ringwood, Victoria, Australia
Penguin Books Canada Ltd, 2801 John Street, Markham, Ontario, Canada L3R 1B4
Penguin Books (N.Z.) Ltd, 182–190 Wairau Road, Auckland 10, New Zealand

Penguin Books Ltd, Registered Offices: Harmondsworth, Middlesex, England

First published in 1989 by Viking Penguin, a division of Penguin Books USA Inc.

1   3   5   7   9   10   8   6   4   2

Library of Congress Cataloging-in-Publication Data
Smith, Doris Buchanan. Voyages
Doris Buchanan Smith. p. cm.
Summary: While immobilized in a hospital bed, Janessa journeys
into a world of dreamlike adventures with the gods of Norse legend.
ISBN 0-670-80739-7   [1. Mythology, Norse—Fiction.   2. Fantasy.]   I. Title.
PZ7.S64474Vo   1989   [Fic]—dc20   89-9175

Printed in the United States of America.
Set in Sabon.

For Bill Curtis,
with whom I have embarked
on an enchanting voyage

VOYAGES

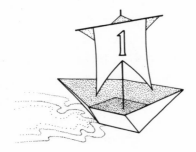

The morning sun slanted through the window and stabbed her eyes. Instantly, it seemed, a nurse was there, lowering the blinds to shut out the sun.

"I want them open," Janessa said.

The blinds flashed semaphore signals as the nurse tried to adjust them to keep the sharp light from Janessa's eyes. For these few minutes, though, the sun would come in. The nurse closed the blinds and blanked the window.

"No-o-o-ooo," Janessa wailed.

"I'll come back in a few minutes and reopen them," the nurse said. Janessa's cry was to a retreating back. The nurse padded away on feet as quiet as pussy willows, leaving the door open when it was supposed to be shut. Janessa sighed. The nurse probably thought the open door was a promise of a prompt return. Sometimes the nurses bobbed in and out so often—taking blood or blood pressure, giving pills or fluffed pillows—that Janessa wished they'd go away. Other times they stayed away for so long she became fearful and pressed the nurse-call button to summon them, to be sure they were still there, guarding.

It had been on television about her, Janessa Kessel. Which fool had told her that? As if she cared about her broken body being on the nightly news. She was in that body when it was snatched from the doorway of the minute market, shoved into the robber's car and later shoved from it. There was no separating the terrors—being grabbed, being in the car with him, or being thrown from it, body tumbling toward swiftly moving pavement. The terror was lodged there, like a persistent seasickness, in spite of being bound, nearly immobile, to this bed. The terror lurked there behind her eyes, stinging, until sometimes she cried her own salt sea. Three weeks hadn't diminished her fear. All the love and assurances from Mom and Dad and all the cards and letters from family, friends, and strangers had not lessened it.

Only here was she safe, pinioned to the bed, weights and pulleys attached to one leg, Crutchfield tongs to her head. She didn't hate it as much as they thought, in spite of the pain. She was safe here. Through the window of this fifth-floor room she couldn't even see treetops to remind her there was a world out there. Cloistered in this room with nurses guarding in the hall, she was safe.

At first someone was with her constantly, Mom or Dad or Grandma or Granddad. Now they were trying to wean her. Her grandparents had gone back to Oregon, which was about as far as you could get from the coast of Georgia. She hated being alone and wanted Mom, Dad, Grandma, Granddad with her. All of them. Some of them. At least one of them.

Now the nurse had closed the blinds. Without the sun, her eyeballs felt like ice.

Dr. Gilder whizzed in, closing the door behind him. "Doors closed, window blinds open," he said, and he crossed the room and opened the blinds. "The sunlight is the color of your hair."

As the sun struck her face she felt her eyes shrink.

Immediately he was at her bedside, sliding sunglasses out of his pocket and onto her face. "You do want the blinds open, don't you? Your window on the world?"

She liked him, then, his knowing she wanted the sun on her face, wanted to see out this window where sky was all she could see, all she wanted to see.

"Are you going to make me something today?" he asked.

"No," she said, watching his face carefully.

"Oh, okay," he said.

"I don't have to make you anything," she said, waiting for his reaction.

"No, of course you don't," he said. "How are you today?"

She shrugged, though the apparatus attached to her head

as traction for her broken back diminished her shoulder movements. Her shrugs were barely noticeable and her nods were invisible. What he wanted to know was what she was thinking, because that's what he was here for, to try to see inside her mind, to probe around her brain as the orthopedic surgeon probed her flesh and bones.

"Do you have it?" she asked. She had, at least, this one daily question.

His daily answer was to remove the fat cylindrical television horizontal output tube from the pocket of his khaki jacket. She liked him for this, too, though she didn't quite admit it to herself. She didn't want to like anyone. She wanted to hate everyone, blame everyone for not protecting her. Dr. Gilder, though, had given her this one small protection from the people who kept turning on the television because they thought it would amuse her or occupy her mind. Only Dr. Gilder really understood her fierce dread of the world. She did not want to see the world—through a window or a television screen. She did not want to hear about how family and friends were doing, or what was going on in the neighborhood, school, town, or world. Hearing about anything reminded her that at any moment someone might be grabbed from a store, taken by a stranger, thrown from a car. Even the Three Stooges, Tom and Jerry, Roadrunner and Coyote were always chasing and framming, bamming and blamming one another. She couldn't bear any of it.

Dr. Gilder was tossing the horizontal output tube into the air, letting it fall through a circle he formed with his arms, then breaking the circle to catch it. "I used to play basketball," he said. "Did I ever tell you that?"

No, he never had. If the tube had fallen and smashed against the floor she would have been immensely satisfied.

"You ever play basketball?"

No, she hadn't, but she didn't say so. She used to run like the wind, and she wasn't going to tell him that, either. But as swiftly as the thought came, so did the burning in her nose and eyes. Quickly, she pulled her workboard into position above her and tugged the utility table closer so she could reach the origami papers.

"It's all right to cry," he said, pulling a chair to her bedside.

The top paper was red-orange. She pressed it against the workboard and folded and folded and flipped and pulled. Had her parents told him how much she cried? She cried when they left, because they were leaving. She cried when they came because they'd been away. Sometimes she cried when they weren't there because they weren't there. And cried when they were there because they were there. But she hadn't cried in front of Dr. Gilder. She handed him a red-orange peony.

"Beautifulllll," he said, sniffing it as though it had a fragrance. Seeing that the sun had left her face, he removed the sunglasses and put them on himself. His eyes went blank behind the one-way reflective lenses. With the help of the sidepiece, he tucked the flower behind his ear.

He looked so silly that amusement ruffled somewhere deep inside her.

"Ah-ha," he said, waggling a finger at her. "I almost got you that time. I saw you have to clamp your throat to keep that smile from coming up. You know, Janessa, it's okay to smile, too."

Holding his arms out as though he had a dancing partner, he twirled around the room, then out, snagging the door with his foot so it closed behind him. Through the door, Janessa heard laughter in the hall.

She clipped the origami book to the overhead work-board, open to the next page. A rabbit. She fingered through the papers for a white sheet and began to learn the folds. She had never even heard of origami, the Japanese art of paper folding, until Grandma had brought her this book and the boxful of vivid papers. Pulling out the ears, feet, and stubby tail of the rabbit was fun. Careful not to tear the paper, she pushed the tail, feet, and ears back into the folds, unfolded the rabbit, and practiced refolding.

Instead of continuing to practice with the same paper, as she usually did, she made another rabbit. Then another, and another. She folded white, blue, purple, brown rabbits and pulled feet, ears, tails from yellow, green, orange, gold rabbits.

When the door opened and she cut her eyes toward it, she was surprised to see fuchsia and pink instead of nurse's white. "Oh," she said when the person got closer. "It's your day."

"If it's Tuesday, it must be my day," said Ms. Simpson, the visiting teacher who had started coming last week.

Twice a week. Of the many routines Janessa was used to, this one was not set in her head yet. Besides, if something didn't happen every day—like bedpans and sheet changes—it was hard to keep track. She hadn't remembered this was Tuesday, wouldn't have remembered Ms. Simpson if she had known it was Tuesday.

"That's quite a proliferation," Ms. Simpson said of the rabbits, as she advanced toward the bed.

Janessa clenched her teeth. "Proliferation" was certain to become a vocabulary word.

"How many do you have?"

Undoubtedly, the rabbits would also proliferate into seventh-grade math problems. Janessa wondered if visiting teachers were told to wear bright cheerful colors and speak in bright cheerful voices. She wasn't cheered. If she'd been in the mood to be amused it would be amusing to watch Ms. Crimson Simpson search for something to interest her. She wished she could run away and, since she could not, she was tempted to put her fingers in her ears. That, however, would be childish and they treated her too much like a baby anyway, with their kindergarten-teacher voices. She would make herself deaf in some other way while Ms. Simpson poured information into her as though she were a soup pot.

Today it was the days of the week. Janessa left both ears open so Ms. Simpson's words would flow through. She decided to think of all the words she knew for reds and pinks.

"The Romans named the days of the week after the planets, including the sun and the moon, for Sunday and Monday," Ms. Simpson said.

Moonday, Janessa thought. Magenta, maroon, she said to herself.

"Mars, Mercury, Jupiter, Venus, and Saturn," Ms. Simpson continued.

Janessa moved on to rose and salmon.

"Saturn for Saturday," the teacher said. "The Saxons kept the days named after the sun and moon and Saturn, but they changed the others to the equivalent Norse gods."

Oh, yes, Janessa thought, letting the words flow through so they wouldn't stick. This was the continuation of the Viking and Norse unit they'd started at school just before she was hurt, combining literature and history and geography into one study package.

"Later the English kept these names," Ms. Simpson droned on. "Tyr became our Tuesday, Woden Wednesday, Thor Thursday, and Frigg Friday."

Norse. Norway. On the day before she'd been hurt, there'd been an avalanche in Norway. Seven people had been killed. If there were such things as gods, why didn't they stop avalanches that killed people? Or keep people from being snatched from stores and thrown from moving cars?

"How did they get Friday from Frigg?" she asked sourly, to distract herself.

"Many of the gods and goddesses were called by different names, and she was also called Frija. Such as you might be called Jan, or Nessa."

"No!" Janessa said sharply. She didn't say that her father affectionately called her Messa until she'd demanded he stop, now that she was such a real mess.

"Woden was also called Odin, and he was the chief god and was also called the All-Father. He had a gold ring from which eight new rings dropped every ninth day."

Janessa rolled her eyes. She'd slipped up and revealed she was listening. Scarlet, she thought. Ruby.

"Frigg is the wife of Odin and is the Queen of Heaven," said Ms. Simpson. "And perhaps you have heard about Thor's hammer. Whenever he throws it, it hits what he aims for and comes back to his hand, like a boomerang. Thor, with his hammer, is the one who makes thunder."

Janessa liked the idea of Thor out there somewhere, banging his hammer to make thunder. A job she'd like herself. Perhaps he was going to make some now. Behind Ms. Crimson Simpson the sky had turned gray. She wasn't satisfied with any of the words she thought of for gray until she thought of smoke. Yes. Smoke was good.

"Tyr, well, uh, he was one-armed and Tuesday is named after him. And that's all I know about Tyr."

Janessa touched a finger to her tongue, nudged a sheet of folding paper from the stack, and resumed making rabbits. "Would you like a red one?" she asked.

"Yes, thanks," Ms. Simpson said. "Do you think you could make a million rabbits? Very few people have any comprehension of what a million really is."

"A vermilion?" Janessa said, handing Ms. Simpson the red rabbit.

"Very goo-ood," Ms. Fuchsia Puchsia said. "I like the rabbit and your wit."

"I can't make a million," Janessa said, continuing the lineage of rabbits. "There were only five hundred papers and I've already used a lot. But I can imagine a million. A million rabbits would fill this bed, fill the room, and start hopping out the door and out the window."

"Indeed they would," Ms. Simpson said, smiling. Then she rumbled on with math, science, geography while the rabbits proliferated from Janessa's hands. "Is there anything you want to ask about your previous assignments?" Ms. Simpson said at last.

"No, ma'am," Janessa said.

"Well, here are your new ones." The teacher set them in the work tray, on top of the origami papers.

Janessa slid her fingers under them for a new origami paper. This one was pink. There were no other words she could think of for pink. She thought of offering this rabbit to Ms. Simpson because it matched her clothes better than vermilion.

"I'll see you Friday, then," the teacher said, dark hair in tight, neat curls, face creamy with makeup and lips which matched the fuchsia skirt. "You know," she said from the doorway. Except for Dr. Gilder, they always stopped in the doorway for some last remark. "You can live inside yourself forever if you want to, Janessa. No one can make you come out."

As soon as the door was closed, Janessa lifted the assignment sheets and put them under the origami papers along with the ones from last week.

Idly, Janessa continued folding rabbits while the lunch tray was carried in. Perhaps she would begin to like Tuesdays and Fridays, she thought, with Ms. Simpson closing the gap between Dr. Gilder and lunch. Mother would be on her way now. She wondered if she could learn to make a rabbit without looking. Closing her eyes, she folded and pulled by feel. Though a bit lopsided, the rabbit turned out okay.

The array of rabbits stopped Mom two paces inside the door.

"I'm impressed!" Mom said, then she continued to the bed and nuzzled Janessa.

Mom's arrival was as satisfying as making rabbits with her eyes closed. She cried with relief to have Mom here.

"You'll have to eat dessert first," Mom said. "I've brought ice cream. Your favorite." Mom tucked a towel under Janessa's chin and across her chest.

She'd had to learn how to swallow lying down. Food was accustomed to traveling through the body vertically, not horizontally. Twice she'd choked frightfully, and whoever was feeding her had to wait for her to be ready. The Heimlich maneuver was not good for a tractioned patient with a broken back.

"Peppermint?" she asked, after the first swallow.

"What do you mean, peppermint?" Mom said. "Of course peppermint. Come on, another bite. That's a good girl."

The next bite was already in, and she had to ignore the

baby tone of her mother's words and concentrate on swallowing. She didn't taste peppermint, but the ice cream did seem doubly cold and there were bits of something crunchy.

"I like your scarf," Janessa said, to get away from the babyness.

Mother spooned more ice cream, then flipped the long tails of the peacock-blue chiffon scarf which floated momentarily before settling back against the khaki suit. Mother always wore a scarf, around her head, around her waist, around her neck. Today she was formal, in that suit.

"Beans, French fries, and steak fingers," Mom said, pulling the lunch tray over, now, and indicating the location of each item. "Do you want to try them yourself?"

"Yes, ma'am," Janessa said, and scrabbled around the plate for a piece of steak. This self-feeding always got messy. No wonder they treated her like a baby.

"So, who are you doing business with today?" Janessa said, poking more food into her mouth, ready to chew while Mom answered.

"Oh, Janny," Mom said, waggling an index finger which meant "Finish chewing and swallow." "I think I've just landed a good new account."

"Billboards?" Janessa asked, for that's what gave her a kick, seeing billboards her mother had thought up and designed. Like the one for United Way with stick figures helping one another all around the border and, in the center, the words, "When we get together, we all have a better way. The United Way."

"Several," Mother said, feeding Janessa a French fry.

"What's the account?" Janessa said, holding her hand up as a signal for Mom to stop feeding her. The food today was easy enough to manage.

Mother licked her lips and made mouth motions to encourage Janessa to chew and swallow. "I don't want to say yet. It's not confirmed. I did my presentation this morning and they really liked it and said they'd call this afternoon."

Janessa said, "Oh," and Mother poked three beans into the openmouthed "oh" before Janessa was ready and Janessa sputtered them out.

"Janessa!" Mother jumped back as flecks of green spattered suit and scarf.

"I'm sorry, I'm sorry," Janessa said, immediately remorseful, ashamed, especially because she'd done it on purpose, to protest being fed.

"No, sweetheart, no. I'm sorry. I shouldn't have been rushing you." Mother wiped Janessa and the bedclothes, then went to the sink to wipe herself.

I wouldn't have done it if you'd said you were on your way to the presentation, Janessa thought with a sigh. She tried so hard to choose things she could manage for herself from the daily menu selection. But people insisted on helping where she didn't want help, feeding, bringing sedatives, opening doors and closing window blinds, and turning on the TV until Dr. Gilder had disabled it. Now Mom's khaki suit, clean of green specks, was dotted dark by water spots.

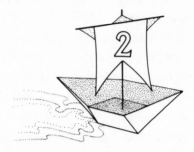

When Mother left, tears traced down the sides of her face. By the little clock Daddy had stuck to the underside of the traction bar above her, it was 12:50, the time Mother always left. Still, it seemed Mother had left early because of her behavior. She had protested being treated like a baby by spitting out her food just like a baby! Now Mother was gone and the afternoon would be so long.

Maybe she would cry all afternoon. There would be deep tracks from the corners of her eyes to her ears where so much water had traveled. Gullies. She reached up to see if they'd started yet and bumped into the Crutchfield tongs.

Bored into the bone. Which fool had told her that? She would rather not have known. There was so much from these past three weeks she would rather have not known. All these bars, braces, weights, and pulleys above and around her looked more like apparatus for athletic training than for keeping one twelve-year-old attached to a bed.

The dull pain of her leg, her back, her head droned like an electronic buzz. She was better, she knew she was better. She knew that last week she was still crying and whimpering at the pain of sheet changing and of having the almost flat bedpan slid beneath her, and now she was not. But last week was behind a curtain, behind the same curtain where she ran like the wind. Today was today's pain and today's fear. She felt no levels of "better than" yesterday, or last week, or the week before.

"Still on rabbits?" said the nurse, making her hourly "look-in."

Janessa held out a blue one. The nurse thanked her and tucked it, head sticking out, into the pocket of her white uniform. She plumped the pillow beneath Janessa's good leg, turned it to the cool side, and padded silently out.

Suddenly Janessa was finished with rabbits. She unclipped the origami book, turned the page, and reclipped. A boat. The next paper was brown. She frowned. For all her complaints about Ms. Fuchsia Puchsia's clothes, she liked the bright colors best. A plain brown boat matched her plain brown mood too well. She wanted chartreuse or cerise, but she didn't reach for another paper. Holding the paper against the work surface she began following the instructions. It was a fine ship, with a mast and a sail. Pulling out the mast and the sail without tearing the paper took all the skill she had acquired through many foldings of peonies and rabbits. Who was clever enough to think up these complicated folds, tucks, and pullouts? she wondered. Admiring the ship, she sailed it back and forth through the air, playing with it as she had played with things when she was younger, her mind floating along with the ship. After a while, she tucked in the sail and lowered the mast to unfold it, to practice refolding.

No sooner had she undone two folds than the ship began to unfold itself, bloop, bloop, bloop, and bloop, as though it were made from a sheet of origami paper larger than the room. The room itself expanded, the walls backing away from this enormous unfolding, as Janessa herself gasped and pressed her elbows into the bed in an attempt to back up from it. Before she could yell or reach for the nurse-call button at the side of the bed, the unfurling stopped and a large, whiskered man leaned over the side of the enormous ship and lifted her aboard.

"Gladden, gladden, grace to you for getting me out," he said, setting her down, feet first, and bowing. "Never before have I fold mitself inside."

"Where did you come from?" she asked, surprised that her words sounded normal and didn't screech.

"I've sailed the great ship *Skidbladnir* for many spans. Great ship, aye? Mit own ship. But no handle inside. Only mistake I know Elves of Ivaldi ever make. Should be latch inside."

"But where did you come from?" Janessa repeated, expecting him to tell her he'd come from her dreams, for surely she'd fallen asleep, as she had on many long, dull hospital afternoons. That would account for this ship being in the room even though it was larger than the room, and the room going tilt to accommodate the ship.

"I am great god Freyr," he said.

"Why do you call everything great?" she asked.

"I am," he said. "We are."

"We who?" She looked down at herself, at her legs, her feet. Her body was normal, unbroken.

"We gods from Norse kingdom of Asgard."

"Ohhh." She had indeed fallen asleep and was dreaming about what Ms. Simpson had told her about the Norse gods and the days of the week. Freyr. It rhymed with fire. He must be the one for Friday.

"Who are you? Where you come from?" he asked, glancing over the side as if to see where he was.

"I'm Janessa. I come from here. Hanover, Georgia, U.S.A."

He looked as astounded as she must have looked when this ship opened up from a tiny paper boat. "Earth? In name of Odin how get mitself to Midgard?" He was rubbing his beard and still looking over the railing. "What happened you?"

In the instant he asked the question, she realized she was standing alone, free from restraints. She touched her head. No Crutchfield tongs. No shaved sides. She moved her head, and it moved. This was the first good dream she'd had and she wanted to stay inside it forever. Gingerly, she took a step. And another. She was her three-weeks-ago normal self, and she ran and leaped and twirled across the deck of this great ship *what?*

"What happened you?" he asked again.

"Nothing. Nothing," she said, ecstatic. Oh, she had known it was a dream, a nightmare, the worst dream she'd ever had. Those awful things, those were the dreams. She had known she would wake up and it wouldn't be true. This strange man, Freyr, was still looking over the railing and she scampered to his side and looked over the railing.

At herself.

She gasped.

There was Janessa, tonged and tractioned, lying in bed with a small, brown, partially unfolded paper boat in her hands. Here was Janessa, standing at the railing of this large wooden ship. What was that story, she wondered, about the boat that ferried people across the river from life to death?

"Am I dead?" she asked, startled and incredibly sad.

"No, no," he said quite pleasantly. "Not now. Not here." He pointed at her. "Not there." He pointed to the Janessa in bed.

The dream was becoming a nightmare. "I, uh, think I want to get off," she said, and started to climb over the rail.

"No!" he said, quickly reaching for her. But she was already over and hung there, stuck and in pain. Hoisting her gently, he lifted her back aboard where she was whole again.

"I don't think I like this," she said. "How can I be in two places at once?"

"All are. More than two. All time is one. Come. I show you mit burial mound," he said, and he turned toward the window and the sails of the ship filled as though from a breeze.

"No-o-o!" she cried, filled with terror. What was dream? What was real? "I want to get off."

"Aye," he said, and he lifted her, lowered her, and put her back into her one self. "Gladden, gladden, grace be with you," he said. The window broadened into an odd curve, as if stretched by a wide-angle lens, and that enormous ship sailed through and off into the smoke-gray sky. As Janessa stared, the clouds billowed to open a peephole of clear blue and, as the boat sailed through, the clouds fell back as though the ship and the slot in the sky had never been.

In the wake, a whoof of a draft scooped origami papers from the top of the box and set them gliding about the room. Paper rabbits hopped all over, including off the bed. Janessa mashed the call button and a nurse came hurrying, colliding with a rose-colored paper drawn toward the door in the crosscurrents.

"What in the world!" the nurse said, jumping as the door banged against the wall behind her. A lavender paper slid with a *shush-sh* into the hall. "Who in the world opened this window?" The nurse crossed the room and one lemon-yellow paper followed the draft right out the window before she could snap it shut. The escaped paper, sun bright on the dusky air, dipped out of sight. Inside, the airborne papers lost wind. Tan and tangerine, amethyst and aquamarine, rose and royal, they zigzagged gracefully to dresser top, Janessa top, and floor.

"Who in the world opened that window?" the nurse repeated. "For sure, you didn't. I wish you could."

"Dr. Gilder," Janessa said, as much to herself as to the nurse. "Dr. Gilder must have opened it when he opened the blinds." She did and she didn't like her origami papers drifting about the room like that. They added to the unreality of having such a quick, strange, daytime dream. Somehow she didn't think she'd been asleep. Somehow, awake, she conjured it.

The nurse gathered the papers, tapped them against the worktable to make a straight stack, and replaced them in the box. Then she fluffed the pillow beneath Janessa's good leg and touched a soft hand to the side of her face.

"You okay?"

Janessa made the invisible nod. Then said, "Uh-huh." This lifelong habit of responding with head movements was useless in the grip of Crutchfield tongs. She wanted the nurse to go, but wanted her to leave the hand at the side of her face, touching.

"May I have a rabbit?"

They'd all stopped hopping. Janessa closed eyes and ears against the kindergarten tone of voice. Even her parents used it. And Grandma. They hadn't talked to her that way before. Voices the color of Ms. Simpson's clothes. Voices as light and colorful as floating origami papers. Only Dr. Gilder talked to her like she was, well, twelve. She liked his somber midnight colors, from hair and face to running shoes. She clutched a handful of rabbits and held them out to Ms. Nurse.

"How about this black one?" she said, copying the cloying voice, sliding one black rabbit out of the clutch.

"Anything else I can do for you?" the nurse said, still syrupy, as she took and admired the rabbit. "You want the door open?"

"No-o-o!" Janessa said. The nurse went out and the door closed with its air-displacing sigh.

The door was supposed to be closed. Janessa liked knowing the nurses were out there, going back and forth, being vigilant, but she didn't want to see anyone except those few who were supposed to come through that door.

Suddenly she was light and free with the memory of the dream, running across the deck of the great wooden ship. She closed her eyes to hold the image and tears squeezed out and dripped toward her ears. Her fist closed tight on the rabbits in her hand.

Running. She had been such a runner, she and her best friend, Lynn. Swift and fleet, beating all comers, they won medals and trophies at the Rec Park track meets. She loved the wind in her face, her hair flowing out behind. Would she ever run again? Would she walk? The doctors said she would, the various doctors, including Dr. Gilder, who was a psychiatrist, a doctor of the mind. To think she might never run again was unbearable. And to think she might was also unbearable, the thought of having to walk again in the world where avalanches and thieves could break up bodies.

Lynn, Lynn, Lynn. Once they had been inseparable. Now she didn't even want to see her. She looked across the room at the huge basket Mom had brought. It was filled to overflowing with cards and letters from people who wished her well. Something every day from Lynn, and she didn't even look at them. Lynn wanted to come see her and she just kept saying, "No, not yet. Please. Not yet." Not ever, she thought now. Not Lynn, not her little sister and brother. Only Grandma, Granddad, Mom, Dad, and Dr. Gilder. She wanted to get well, be off this bed. She did. But she wanted to live in this hospital room forever.

She rummaged around among the rabbits, trying to find the paper boat. Perhaps she could construct her own world. What a strange and frightening feeling it had been to be aboard that ship and see herself aboard the bed. Ms. Simpson said she could live inside herself as long as she wanted. And she had been doing that, these past three weeks. But she'd been living there dully and unresponding, closing things out, even the taste of peppermint. Would it be possible to create daydreams that would be as vivid and real as sleep dreams? As vivid and real as that ship and the funny, whiskered man? During the few minutes on that ship, she'd been healed and whole. She moved the overhead mirror so she could see the bed, but the boat was either lost among the rabbits or had fallen to the floor. Or had it really become that larger boat and flown out the window and into the sky? Would she dare to make another one?

Well, it didn't have to be a boat, she thought. She could think of something else. But could she control it? That was the key. She'd had times, even while dreaming, when she knew she was dreaming. Still, dreams suddenly went off at odd angles. Like this one today. Happily running along the deck of the ship and seeing herself in bed at the same time. And him, Freyr, talking about showing her his tomb when there he was, obviously alive and well. She didn't want nightmares. She'd had enough of those.

What she wanted was something like the dream she sometimes had about flying with a coat hanger. It was just an ordinary wire coat hanger out of the closet, but with the smallest push-off leap she was in the air, the hook of the hanger leading the way, she controlling direction by tilting the hanger. Those were always good dreams, happy dreams, floating, soaring, flying dreams. In those dreams, even though she'd never actually flown, she'd seen Hanover from above. The roof of her own house, and Lynn's, and the rounded top of the water tower, and the switchback tidal creeks in the marshes between Hanover and Golden Isle.

Yes, she thought. That's it. She would create her own world. No rooftops. No water towers. Just marsh and water and a nugget of an island for her to land on when she came down from flying. No people. She didn't want people. Not even in the dreamworld.

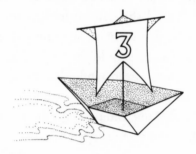

Instead of thinking up daydreams, she started marking the time until her parents came, ticking off every dragging minute, ready to cry if they didn't show up when they were supposed to.

Perched on the edge of time, she fell off into tears when Dad walked in. Five-ten on the dot. Bankers walked out of their offices precisely at five o'clock. Even vice-presidents. The cello case hung from his right hand and from his left hand floated a string which tethered a silver foil balloon. He set the cello down and stooped and leaned for sweet hugs.

"Isn't this yours? And how did it get outside?" He showed her the yellow origami paper which had sailed out the window.

"We had a draft," she said, holding him, sniffles subsiding, hugging him, wanting to make him lean there, hugging, forever.

"Draft enough to make this travel around the room, I hope," he said, releasing the balloon which rose, bumped into and scuffed along the ceiling. On the side opposite the silver foil was a hot pink smiley face. It reminded Janessa of Ms. Fuchsia Puchsia and every too-cheery person who walked into this room.

"Daddyy-y-y," she said, ready to tell him to get that baby balloon out of here. But his face was like the balloon face, pink and smiling. Telling him she didn't like it would be like sticking a pin in his face.

"I can do origami, too, see?" he said, folding the yellow paper into a small, peaked hat and perching it atop his curly red hair. "Checkers?" He reached to a bottom drawer for the checkerboard.

He might be smiling now but she knew she wasn't the only one who cried. She'd seen him work his mouth against crying, heard him not get words out past the lumps in his throat. Would she have protested about the balloon if Mom had brought it? Would she have spewed green beans all over Dad if he was irritating her with baby talk? If she said she didn't like the balloon, he would take it out of here, but he would probably give it to someone else, and she didn't want it scurrying along the ceiling anywhere in this hospital. She wanted it destroyed. Dr. Gilder would pop it for her if she asked. Just so Daddy didn't know.

He set the checkerboard across her stomach and perched a rabbit on each corner. "The judges," he said. His wrist and white shirt cuff bobbed in and out of the sleeve of his suitcoat as he arranged the checkers. When they began the game, he looked at the board and she looked at the mirror above her which looked at the board for her. They'd barely begun when the dinner tray came.

"Please let me eat by myself," she said.

"Okay," he said, "but let me finish the game first. I'm winning." The fact was they'd just begun and nobody was winning yet. But he made illegal jumps all over the board until he'd jumped all her checkers. "Shall I remove the rabbits or are you feeding them?"

"Ohhh, Daddy-y-y," she said.

He whisked the checkerboard away and gathered armfuls of rabbits and put them everywhere—on the dresser, the chairs, the windowsill, and perched them precariously between the slats of the window blinds. He spread a towel across her and rolled the tray table over. Dinner was pizza, and no matter how careful she tried to be, the toppings topped her as she struggled to maneuver from tray to mouth.

"Hey, I believe your mother could make a shirt design using this theme," Dad said. "Olive on the chin. Pepperoni on the nose."

If she was in the mood for anything funny, this would

be funny. But she hadn't found anything funny since the day at the store. Certainly there was nothing funny about this green Jell-O. Had she ordered Jell-O? There was no way to eat it without feeling like a baby. Either you used your hand to hold the wiggly stuff onto the spoon or you let someone feed you.

"Do you want me to . . . ?" Daddy began to ask.

"No, Daddy." Then after a minute she said, "Will you, please, Daddy?" Still, it made her want to cry, but she couldn't cry and eat. The very idea of wanting to cry over Jell-O made her want to cry double.

Afterwards, when he had cleared away and washed her up and even brushed her hair a little, she settled back for the concert. She was already settled back, of course, could do nothing but settle back. But when he brought the cello, there was music and she'd known this music, his music, all her life. The resonance of bow against strings was such a beloved and familiar sound it was grafted onto her bone, fused with her spirit. She closed her eyes and absorbed the sweet, safe sound.

Others might think it odd, him playing the entire cello part of the Brandenburg Sixth as though it were a solo. But she heard the other strings inside her head. When he stopped she didn't open her eyes for a minute, didn't want to open her eyes. She was traveling somewhere inside the music in a way, she supposed, that he, too, was inside the music. But lest he think she was asleep and slip away, she opened her eyes and there was Mom. Nice. No one had slipped away. Someone had slipped near instead.

"Mmmm, nice, eh?" Mom said, coming over to nuzzle and hug.

The room was so full of good feeling that for the first time Janessa thought maybe, if she could hold this good feeling and wrap it all around herself, then maybe sometime, still a long time from now, she might be able to leave this room. If only Mom didn't ruin it by saying something about how Dad should have been a professional musician instead of burying himself in Hanover.

"Did you tell Daddy about your new account?" she asked, as a diversion. Tonight Mom's scarf was around her head, tied at the side and hanging long behind one shoulder.

"You have a new account? Great," Dad said, coming close and making a three-way nuzzle.

"No, I haven't told him yet," Mom said. "I'm just now seeing him. He came directly here, to you, and I went home to see about Donna and Billy. I have a surprise for you."

Janessa liked them touching her, keeping a hand on her hair, her face, her shoulder, her arm, holding her hand. But she didn't like their surprises. It took Dr. Gilder's removing the horizontal output tube to make them quit surprising her with video cartoons they thought were funny. She had never noticed before how much comedy was made from pain. These characters were constantly trouncing one another or banging into things. Bodily pain was no longer amusing.

"I brought you some pictures," Mom said.

Even faster than Mom could fan the pictures, Janessa closed her eyes. "This was the day Billy and Donna got into a jam fight," Mother said, describing the pictures. "What a mess! And, look, Billy finally made it up the pear tree without your help."

Tears eked out.

"And here's old Putter," Mom continued, just as though Janessa were looking. They thought she missed her brother and sister and the dog, and that homesickness was what made her cry. They didn't understand that even the good news reminded her of the bad news, the bad things that happened to people. Pictures and even mention of her darling butter-haired sister and brother, who were small enough to be adored, were too painful. What if something happened to them? How could she bear it? And mention of the soft, scruffy-haired dog reminded her of all the moving vehicles he could run in front of. Maybe even one driven by a robber who'd kidnapped a girl. Or innocent people with skis on top of the car who were, after hitting the dog, going to get themselves whumped by an avalanche.

"Didn't Dr. Gilder tell you?" she said, eyes and teeth clenched.

"Tell me what, sweetheart?" Mother said.

Janessa sighed. It was like trying to explain something to Donna and Billy, going around and around because they were too young to understand. Why wouldn't Mom and Dad understand? Or did Dad understand?

He drew the bow across the cello again, making cranky sounds, then vibrating the strings in a rapid trill. "How about some demisemiquavers?" he asked, and he kept demisemiquavering but she didn't open her eyes. Then his lips were brushing her cheek.

"I have to go, baby doll. We're working on Mozart's Quartet for Violoncello and it's tough for us amateurs." He played chamber music for the fun of it with several other good musicians who'd "buried" themselves in Hanover.

"Any demisemiquavers?" she asked, opening her eyes, ready for his kiss.

"Yes," he said, kissing her, picking up the canvas cello case. "Several runs of four. That's one thing that makes it so difficult." She was pleased to have this particular bit of knowledge, that demisemiquavers were thirty-second notes and they were so fast that four of them took up the space of only one quarter note. She almost smiled as he left the room. He was pretty cute, her father, so tall, with curly red hair, and all those freckles. Too bad none of them, Billy, Donna, or herself, had red hair. They all had yellow hair like Mom said hers was when she was young.

"He really could have been a musician, couldn't he?" Janessa said.

"He is a musician," Mom said as she filled a stainless steel bowl with warm water for the evening bath.

"You know what I mean. A professional musician. Instead of a banker."

"Sure," Mom said, beside her now, tucking towels beneath her good leg and soaping, washing, rinsing.

"Why isn't he, then?" She wasn't sure she really wanted

to hear it again. Such comments irritated Daddy and sometimes irritated her for his sake, and now here she was asking for it.

Mother patted that leg dry, tucked towels around the tractioned leg, and moved the warm, soapy cloth with great care. "My, you're into complicated questions this evening." Mother removed the patterned smocked gown, one of several Grandma had made, but still open-backed, like the hospital gowns. How else would they get it on her?

"What's so complicated about it?" she asked. "I've heard you say plenty of times that he should be playing music instead of being stuck in a bank in Hanover."

"You haven't heard me say it lately," Mom said, rinsing and resoaping the washcloth and handing it to Janessa. No one could wash her stomach and sides but herself. She was ticklish and it made her jerk with a spasm even when it wasn't funny.

"Why not?" Janessa said, returning the washcloth to be rinsed, then rinsing the ticklish parts of herself.

Mom wet the cloth again and covered Janessa's face with it and gently cleaned her face, including the stiff, salty track of dried tears. "Each of us has to choose for ourselves. Even those who love us can't choose for us." Mom held the washcloth to the side of her face, looking at her, saying more with silence than she had with words, transferring the subject of the conversation from Daddy to Janessa, or so Janessa thought, until Mother continued. "Let's don't talk about it, okay? The subject makes him mad and it makes me sad." Janessa almost blinked in surprise. She'd thought the musing, with the washcloth at the side of the face, was about her, but apparently they were still talking about Daddy. "Did he bring you that silly balloon?" Mom stood, swung the washcloth high, swatted the smiley balloon in its smiley face, and it skittered backwards along the ceiling. She stretched out her thumbs and tucked them under her chin to frame her face, her mouth in a huge clownish grin. "Smile, smile, smile?" she said, bobbing her framed face to imitate the nodding balloon. "No one can be sad in this room."

Janessa was amazed. Mother understood. Maybe they could talk about it. But Mother tugged at Janessa's big toe and said, "This little pig went to market," and closed the moment.

After Mom left, Janessa noticed a snapshot of Donna and Billy and Putter clipped to the work surface above her. In anger, she reached up and pulled it down. Then she didn't know what to do with it. Tearing it up was like doing something awful to Donna and Billy. Sailing it across the room wasn't much better. She didn't want it clipped above her, or where she'd keep coming across it in her things on the extra tray table. Finally she put it on the bed beside her ear, but she felt their images as surely as though they were crawling through her ear to get inside her head. Reaching for it, she bumped it out of reach and out of sight from the overhead mirror. So they perched there, somewhere on the corner of her bed, as the rabbits had perched on the corners of the checkerboard, but they radiated warmth and smiles and life. Janessa wished she'd followed her first impulse and torn up the picture.

Perhaps she'd knocked the snapshot to the floor and sometime in the night a nurse retrieved it and reclipped it to the work surface, for when she opened her eyes in the morning, there were Donna and Billy and even Putter, laughing down at her.

Later, while the sun was warm and blinding, Dr. Gilder breezed in with his quick step and slid a pair of sunglasses onto Janessa's face.

"Yours," he said.

"Really?" she said, surprised she hadn't thought to ask for a pair. They would have brought her anything, her parents. But being in the hospital, indoors, she just hadn't thought about sunglasses, even though the sun pierced her eyes for a few minutes each morning. Also, since the uh, incident, abduction—*it,* this thing that had happened to her—her brain had been on malfunction. She sometimes couldn't think of the simplest things. Such as sunglasses. A normal reaction to shock, everyone told her.

"What do we call this?" she asked.

"Sunglasses," he said.

She didn't know if he was trying to be funny or what. "No-o-o," she wailed. "I mean this." She ran her hands down her body. "This thing that happened to me."

"What do you call it?" he asked.

She was so tired of his questions, his trying day after day to find out how she thought and what she felt about things. "Well, it wasn't an accident," she said.

"No, it surely wasn't that."

"But I was thinking that I haven't been thinking clearly since the—the what? I don't know what to call it."

"Well, let's think of some words."

"Incident?" she offered.

"Oh, it was more than an incident, don't you think? Mishap? Calamity? Catastrophe? Injury?" He left spaces between each word but none of these were the right word. "Outrage," he said.

"Yes," she said. "Outrage." That had the hurtful violence in it. "Since the outrage." The sun had gone off her face and she removed the sunglasses to look at them. She almost laughed, or came the closest she'd come in three weeks, since the day she walked so happily home from school and stopped by the store on the way. The sunglasses were ridiculous. "Where did you get these? From Lana Turner?"

"She gave them to me personally," he said. "But how does someone your age know about Lana Turner? I'm not even old enough to know about Lana Turner."

"Old movies," she said. "My parents watch old movies." Lana Turner was an actress with bleached-blond hair and white fur coats and glittery, pointed-corner sunglasses. Janessa put them back on. "Why don't you come in the afternoon instead of the morning?" she asked. She was beginning to enjoy him, and afternoons moved so slowly.

"I have office hours in the afternoon," he said.

His answer astonished her. Yes, of course, she thought. She never heard of a doctor having only one patient but, well, she hadn't thought about him having anyone but her.

In spite of the way he whizzed around, he never seemed in a hurry, and he made her feel special, as though he thought of her only and trusted her to know the right things for herself.

"Afternoons are boring, eh?"

She liked him for knowing. She liked him for not being so everlastingly cheerful. Black clothes. Black hair. Black skin. "Everyone comes in the morning."

"What can we do about that, I wonder. Do you have any ideas?"

She shrugged, her shoulders making their minute movement. "After lunch there's nobody until Mom or Dad can get here after five."

"You think about it," he said, "and so will I. Let's see what we can come up with. A person shouldn't have to lie there bored all afternoon."

"I could count to a million," she said, thinking of her "vermilion" quip to Ms. Simpson.

"Could you really?" He laughed. "I couldn't."

Her always upward-looking eyes suddenly caught the snapshot of Donna and Billy. "Didn't you tell my parents?" she asked.

"Tell them what?"

"Not to tell me about home. Not to bring me pictures."

He followed her eyes, leaned over, and looked up. "Who put it there?"

"Mom," she said.

"But you can reach it and take it down, can't you?"

She thought of last night when she'd taken it down and

hadn't been able to decide what to do with it. "Yes, but . . ." Oh, how she missed being able to make a good, huge shrug. She made another small one. "I didn't know what to do with it. I couldn't tear it up and it seemed so hateful to throw it on the floor."

"Shall I put it in my pocket with the output tube? I will, if you want me to. But you will have to hand it to me." He held out his hand.

Janessa reached. But somehow to give him this photo of Donna and Billy to ride around in a dark pocket was like handing them over in person, as though she didn't want them, as though she didn't care. Withdrawing her hand, she said, "I'll give it back to Mom."

When Dr. Gilder left, she began counting and the numbers tumbled off her tongue as fast as when she was counting for hide and seek. She was tempted to slide into the split-second onetwothreefourfivesixseveneightnineTEN, onetwothreefourfivesixseveneightnineTWENTY routine and go up by tens, but if she was going to count to a million she wanted to say every number. She was tongue-tied and cockeyed on 1,213 when a nurse came in for a routine check. Then she couldn't remember the number, but she knew she was over a thousand, so she started there and when it was time for lunch, she wrote down 4,240.

"Where in the world did you get those?" Mother said the moment she came into the room.

"Dr. Gilder," Janessa said. "In the mornings, the sun is in my face for a few minutes, but I don't want the blinds closed."

"Well, wasn't that nice. Chartreuse!" Even before hugging, Mother took the glasses from Janessa, tried them on, and returned them. "Looks like they belong to Lana Turner."

"That's what I told Dr. Gilder," Janessa said. "He was surprised I even knew about Lana Turner." She saw Mother notice that the snapshot was still in place. Chartreuse, she thought. Maybe she would think of all the words she could for green. Mother had on a forest-green blouse with khaki slacks, and tied around her waist, like a pirate, a printed scarf in mint, emerald, and forest green.

The boring afternoon loomed, with nothing to interrupt it but the bedpan, should she need to use it. She lay in bed in her Lana Turner chartreuse sunglasses and counted to 9,930. She was going for ten thousand or bust, but she busted first. All that counting could bore a person, she discovered. It had taken her nearly an hour to get that far. If she counted to twenty thousand every day, she figured it would take her fifty days to count to a million. Wow! That was a lot. She was so tired of lying here. If only she could go somewhere. Yet there was nowhere she wanted to go. Except aboard that ship, maybe, the ship of her imagination where she had run freely up and down the deck. Almost idly she swung the work surface above her and lifted a sheet of origami paper from the worktable. But her fingers didn't know what to do. She had not learned how to make the boat.

Opening the origami book, she clipped it above her and was immediately satisfied. The book covered Billy and Donna. After she folded the paper boat, she held it, wondering what would happen if she unfolded it. Could her imagination create that ship again? As much to prove to herself that she couldn't as that she could, she unfolded the paper boat.

Instantly the prow of the *Skidbladnir* drifted through the closed window. Glass, brick, metal opened and the entire ship floated through the walls as though they were made of air, and the room widened into that odd warp to make space.

"Aye. Gladden, Janessa," the bearded Freyr said, leaning down immediately to lift her up. "You come this time?"

Dizzy from the swell of the room, Janessa swayed a bit on deck as she looked at herself in the yellow gown with smocking which flew open in the back. "I don't have any clothes," she said.

"Garments, lass?" He held out a hand and a smaller but duplicate set of his own clothes appeared in that hand as, with the other, he reached and lifted her to shipboard.

She stepped into the leather breeches and soft-soled boots and slid the tunic over her head as she slipped her arms out of the gown and into the sleeves of the tunic. Everything smelled of ancient wood and old leather. With a flick of her wrist, she tossed the gown overboard where it landed in a heap on the floor. Strange to see Janessa lying there in bed, with a yellow gown, while the same gown lay crumpled on the floor.

"What are those big eyes?" Freyr asked, pointing at her face as the ship eased out the window.

Frowning, she touched her face. "Oh," she said. "Sunglasses." She'd forgotten she had them on. She took them off and held them out.

Taking them, he perched them on his large face. The stems clung to his temples and he had to look cross-eyed to see through the lenses. "Aye. Makes night. Why do you want to make dark?"

"To help me see better if things are too bright."

"Ayyye." He nodded. "Like light from arms of Gerd."

"Gerd?" she asked.

"My wife," he said, holding out his arms. "White arms of Gerd light sky and sea." Goggle-eyed and cross-eyed through sunglasses, he looked dreamy as he thought of his wife, and the *Skidbladnir* moved smoothly through the bright blue air.

"Where do you dwell?" he asked, handing her back the sunglasses and looking over the side of the ship.

Hmmm, she thought. How did he know she didn't live in the hospital room? Ignoring his question, she didn't look over the railing but looked out at the sky. Only when she thought they were too high to see anything below did she look down. They were too high to identify Hanover, if it was Hanover, but there below was a patchwork of earth, green and brown, with ribbons of highways and rivers. The quilted look of earth pleased her. From this distance, she liked it.

Wisps of clouds drifting above them thickened and locked out the sky above. But the clouds whirled until one clear blue circle of sky shone through. The *Skidbladnir* whooshed through the tunnel of clouds which closed behind them like a thick curtain. The view disappeared. All was white below and blue above as they sailed across a sea of clouds that looked like miles of marshmallows or fields of feathers. As she stared, Janessa began to see dimensions in this new white world, cloud hills and plains, clouds rising to be cloud mountains, and occasional depths of blue, like lakes in the clouds.

"It looks like cloud mountains," she said to Freyr.

"Is Ice Mountains. Land of Frost Giants," he said. "We have crossed over."

"Frost Giants?" she said, peering out across the Ice Mountains, looking for shapes. "I don't see any giants," she said, thinking also that she didn't need any giants.

"Same color as mountains. Hard to see," he said. "Look. Hrungnir stalking through pass."

To Janessa, it was the same as looking at the clouds. There was a shifting and a movement which could be a giant as easily as a sheep or a whale or some of the other shapes she often saw in clouds.

Then clouds changed to water the color of robins' eggs

and ahead of them was the largest rainbow she'd ever seen, with the spectrum repeated three or four times. And at the end of the rainbow—what a dream, what a dream! Gold! A city of gold, glinting in the sun.

"Approaching Asgard," Freyr said. "The Rainbow Bridge."

But her attention was snapped away from the colors of the bridge by the sound of clamoring hooves, like the stampedes she'd seen and heard in movies. Racing down a wooded slope, making the noise of hundreds, was one enormous golden boar. The trees laid stalks of shadows across the hill but instead of a shadow below the boar, there was a shining. Snorting gold vapor, the animal reached the edge of the river, bounded into space, and hurtled toward them, pawing air as though it were solid ground.

"Look out!" she yelled in warning to Freyr, and ducked below the gunnel just as the boar soared over her head. After all the rumbling, stampeding sound, it alighted on the deck as silent as a butterfly.

"Goldenbristle," Freyr said, patting and rubbing the animal, ducking from the huge licking tongue. "Aye, lass." He reached a hand out and drew Janessa to the boar's side. "Goldenbristle is gentle beast, honey of tongue and of spirit. Touch."

He guided her hand to touch the beast. "Soft," she said, but pulled her hand away, even as she stared at the light on the deck where a shadow ought to be.

"Finest gold," he said. "Spun by Elves of Ivaldi. Gift from Loki for mischief done."

"Loki?" she said.

"You will meet Loki."

"Elves?"

"You will not meet Elves of Ivaldi. They dwell beneath earth and trust no one. Only mischievous Loki sees them." Freyr shrugged one shoulder. "Loki alone knows Ivaldi language."

The *Skidbladnir* had sailed up to the Rainbow Bridge and seemed, by comparison, like a pea-pod boat.

"Gladden, Freyr. Why do you bring strangers?" boomed a voice from the bridge.

"Aye, gladden, Heimdall, grace be with you. Meet Janessa. One small stranger," Freyr said. "Not strange to me."

"But from Midgard, world of men!" Heimdall said. "I saw you come through hole in clouds."

"Janessa, meet Heimdall, Keeper of Bridge. Heimdall sees to ends of world and hears fruit growing on my trees."

Janessa nodded in awe of such power of sight and sound. A multicolored mist drifted from the bridge and gathered around Heimdall's ankles.

"Does Odin give permission?" Heimdall asked.

"We go to Odin now," Freyr said, lowering the sails. He collapsed the masts like telescopes, folded and tucked things until the great ship was as small as a raft, and Freyr stepped off, looking at her to follow.

"I'll wait here," she said, wondering what would happen if the *Skidbladnir* became a paper boat again. Only the boat was magic. Only here could she leave the reality of lying stiffly on the hospital bed. Goldenbristle had leaped off with Freyr, but now set one foot back on the small boat, tilting it wildly. For balance, Janessa grabbed the spiky bristles that stood up along the boar's back between his shoulder blades. Momentarily, the ship-boat-raft stabilized, then Goldenbristle stepped away from the *Skidbladnir,* with Janessa hanging on.

Several kinds of fear flew into her. The first—that she would be back in the hospital bed injured and helpless—was immediately proved wrong. Goldenbristle stood beside Freyr as Janessa slid off into the glow of his shining and onto her own two strong and working legs. The other fear was not so easily proven.

Was it possible, she wondered, to go so far into the imagination that you couldn't get back?

She turned and looked downriver, as though it was the Altamaha and she could see Hanover from here, but she did not have Heimdall's eyes. She caught no sight of the flatlands of home. All she saw were the rolling hills of this green and gold Asgard, the endless river and the endless distance.

Suddenly there was someone else there, appearing in the air from nowhere. She ducked as though he were landing on her head. Did everyone, everything around here fly or just materialize?

"Who are you?" he asked.

"Who are *you?*" she asked back.

Before either of them could answer, he said, "What are these big eyes?" and plucked the sunglasses off her and put them on himself. As they had with Freyr, they perched small on his large face and he had to look cross-eyed to see through the lenses.

"Gladden, Loki. Meet Janessa," Freyr said. "Janessa, meet Loki."

Loki was busy peering at things—grass, flowers, Goldenbristle's golden hair—as though the glasses were magnifying lenses.

"They're sunglasses," Janessa said.

Loki turned and looked at the sun. "Aye. The sun is more clear because not so bright, aye?" Loki was Freyr's size but beardless, younger, and more slender. Loki gathered a handful of color dust from the Rainbow Bridge and sprinkled it over Janessa's head, peering at it with the sunglasses. Heimdall grumbled his displeasure.

"Loki," Freyr said. "Return Janessa's big eyes now. We go to Odin."

Loki inspected Janessa one more time and disappeared. In his place, a falcon hovered, then flew away across treetops, sunglasses in its beak.

"Loki, I'm warning you," Freyr called.

Janessa clapped a hand over her mouth and quickly moved it between her teeth and bit the side of one finger. Caught between delight and scary strangeness, she thought, I want to be back in my bed right now. When her wish didn't happen immediately, she said it out loud, adding, with all the power that was in her, "Now!"

"Now? We go to Odin now," Freyr said. "Maybe scapegrace Loki bring back big eyes." Shaking his head he said, "I wonder if Freya knows Loki has her falcon shape again?" He reached toward the raft *Skidbladnir* and folded it in half and in half yet again, like folding a sheet.

"No," she said to his back, alarmed that willing herself back to bed had not worked.

He looked back at her. "Apologies for Loki. Always we must apologize for Loki."

"I want to go back now," she said.

"Because of big eyes? If he does not bring back big eyes, I will make you gift. Something fine as big eyes." He kept making the *Skidbladnir* smaller and smaller, until he took it in his hands to finish the final folds. "Come. Odin waits. All strangers of Asgard must meet All-Father promptly."

The longer this continued, the more fascinated and fearful she became. Occasionally when she was waking from a good dream, she could will herself to make it last a little longer, to see what happened. And she was interested to see what would happen, to see what Odin was like. Hadn't Ms. Simpson used the term All-Father, too? Wasn't this Odin for whom Wednesday was named? Odinsday? But this was too scary already, like the day last summer when she and Lynn had floated out from the beach on air mattresses and drifted so far they were afraid of not getting back.

"I need to get back now," she said, trying to contain her fear. Perhaps Freyr himself would turn into a bird and carry her away in his beak. "They'll miss me at the hospital," she added, for emphasis.

He shook his head. "They will not miss. This is all-time, no-time. They will not miss." He opened a pouch fastened to his belt and started to slide the now-four-inch folded boat into it.

All-time? No-time? Could she get lost in time, too? "I have to get back now," she said, and she snatched the small boat from him and frantically pulled and tugged to unfold it, but no magic happened.

Freyr cocked his head slightly. "Aye, a feisty one." He reached out and took back the pouch and the boat. With a few flips, the *Skidbladnir* was restored to sailing trim. "We go."

Janessa bit her lip. Clearly he was disappointed.

They slid away from the dock, sailed the river to the river of clouds, and seemed to sail the clouds forever.

"How will we find our way back?" she asked.

"We keep going. Clouds always end somewhere," he said.

In a moment, there was a break in the clouds which they swooped down through and then in through the hospital window. She ran to the railing and saw herself lying straight out and sleeping in the bed, the yellow gown in a lump on the floor.

"You want to come again, you beckon me," Freyr said. "Grace be with you." He lifted her over and he was away and she was here, away from the no-time and the all-time and into the now-time. Her eyes were open. She wasn't sleeping. She knew where she had been.

Tears welled in her wide-open eyes, mixing the fear of being away with the fear of being back. She punched the call button and cried, "Nurse, nurse, the window!"

A nurse bustled in and over to the window. "Who in the world would leave the window open on such a cold day?"

"Is it cold?" Janessa said, tears moving down the tracks beside her eyes. She hadn't felt cold, either out there or in here.

Turning from the window, the nurse stooped and picked up the gown from the floor.

Two yellow gowns? But Grandma had made only one. Janessa was surprised it had not become one gown, as she had become one Janessa, but not surprised enough to stop crying.

"Aww now, what's the matter?" the nurse asked, smoothing the gown over the back of a chair.

"Would you put my gown in the drawer, please?" Janessa hiccupped, trying to talk while crying. "The second drawer. Under the clean things."

The nurse complied, then reached to touch Janessa's hair. "Feeling lonesome? These long afternoons? Ready to get out of this place? I know."

No, you don't know, Janessa thought. Still, the hand stroking her hair felt so good it made her cry harder.

Now the nurse plumped the pillow beneath Janessa's good leg, always the last move they made before leaving the room. Did they learn that in nursing school? Janessa wondered. "I'll get you a sedative," the nurse said, checking the chart hanging on the end of the bed.

"No-o," Janessa said, but the nurse had padded out on whisper feet. What's wrong with crying? Janessa wanted to say. Why can't a person just cry and keep on crying until she's finished if she wants to? But the firmness of mind required to think the thought squelched the tears so that she was not crying when the nurse came back with a pill in a tiny pleated cup.

Almost without looking, the nurse handed Janessa the pill and held the glass of water beside her, poking the flexible straw toward the corner of Janessa's mouth.

"I'm okay," Janessa said. "I don't want anything."

"Oh, come on. It will make you feel better."

"I don't want it," Janessa said, just barely keeping from knocking pill and water away. What startled her most was realizing what she almost said. She'd almost said, "I *don't want* to feel better."

"Okay," said the nurse. "Let me know if you change your mind." And she was gone again, like a wisp, a vapor.

I don't want to feel better? She let this idea circle for a moment. When I get better, they will make me leave this room. How did things get so muddled? she wondered. Now she wished she had taken the sedative, especially if it would make her go to sleep. What she wanted to do most was to turn on her side, curl up and go to sleep.

"Ha!" she said out loud, about her inability to curl up. But it was not a laughing *ha.*

The rolling sound of the X-ray cart reached her ears a moment before it and Dr. Gilder reached the door in a tie. Dr. Gilder gave her a saluting wave and disappeared as the technicians shoved the X-ray cart into the room. Janessa groaned. She'd rather have Dr. Gilder.

"I know," one of them said tenderly. Yes, Janessa thought with a sigh, they all thought they knew. "I wish we didn't have to do this." One of them pressed on the bed while the other jimmied an X-ray plate into position beneath her.

There ought to be a better way, she thought, as they pushed her aerial work surface aside and swung the machine above her. Why couldn't they set the X-ray plate on top of her and take the X-ray from below, from beneath the bed?

"Be still, now," the guy said, and she was tempted to wave her arms back and forth across her body to mess them up. Be still. Very funny. They pressed the bed down, removed the first plate, and inched the second under. Always two. If she waved her arms and ruined one she'd be messing herself up, not them. She'd just have to undergo the agony again. All this X-ray plates under, bedpans under, and changing sheets didn't seem good for a person with a broken back, but they certainly couldn't put the bedpan over!

At first they'd had something called a catheter attached to her, to drain off her pee. They said, "We know it hurts," but it didn't, or not so she could sort it out from all the other things that hurt. It had been hard, though, just to pee when she had to pee, to just let it go without being on the toilet. She'd expected to feel the bed go wet and warm beneath her, but it didn't. Her pee flowed through a tube or something to who knows where. She'd never asked, hadn't cared, so long as her bed was dry. And the bedpan, so flat it didn't seem as though it could hold a thimbleful, was even harder, feeling the hot pee course down herself until it reached the bedpan. And having someone else wipe her, clean her down there, she hated.

The physical therapist, Kirsten, came in as they were

winding up the X-ray. Another groan escaped Janessa. What awful timing. Sweat would pour off her for an hour just from the ordeal of the X-ray.

"You might as well do all your sweating at once," Kirsten said, as though reading Janessa's mind. "Feeling better? Feeling stronger? By next week, we'll have you home." Kirsten attacked immediately, lifting Janessa's good leg and flexing it to her belly and back, belly and back. Home? Janessa thought. This is my home. "Push against my hand," Kirsten said. "Push."

But it hurt to push. It couldn't be good for a person with a broken back to push against anything. Janessa watched the two people rolling out the X-ray machine, one pushing, one pulling. Did she expect them to stop Kirsten? And why. She was probably as anonymous to them as they were to her. She could not have said if they were or weren't the same two who X-rayed her last week and the week before. Nor did she have the nurses straight, or know their names unless she looked at their name tags, which she usually didn't, though Mother seemed to know them. To Janessa they were just snow women, dressed in white and quiet as snowflakes in their rubber-soled shoes. How come she knew Kirsten's name and not these others? she wondered.

"Still in your rag-doll mode, eh?" said Kirsten, giving the leg some sharp, massaging slaps. "Kick my nose," she said, leaning in range of Janessa's big toe, tapping her nose with her finger. "Come on. Kick my nose."

"I can't," Janessa said.

"Come on, this leg has to be strong to help the other one along as it mends."

Kirsten put the balls in Janessa's hands and Janessa began to squeeze. She used her hands and arms. She wasn't so afraid to do Kirsten's exercises with her hands and arms. Kirsten massaged her shoulders, neck, and even her face.

"Move that face around, Janessa," Kirsten said, moving her own face around in mugging poses. "Move every single muscle that will move. The body wants to be whole and healthy, and if you keep the uninjured parts in good shape, they will help out the injured parts." Last of all, she gently rubbed Janessa's head around the area where the Crutchfield tongs were attached and ohhh, that felt so good, so necessary.

"You'll be back on the track team by spring," Kirsten said.

"What team?" Janessa said suspiciously. She knew they all talked about her, but she didn't want confirmation.

"My little sister is on the track team. Margaret Hall. I told you, remember?" Kirsten kissed her index finger and touched it to Janessa's nose and left the room as quietly as the nurses did. But Kirsten was not in white; maybe that's why she remembered Kirsten and Ms. Simpson. They wore regular clothes. They weren't anonymous in uniforms.

She was soaked in sweat. The gown stuck to her. Gown and skin were cool and clammy. This was when she needed attention. A warm sponge bath and a dry gown and a cover across her. Where were all the bustling bodies when you needed them? A person could catch pneumonia right here in the hospital. Still, she didn't press the nurse-call button.

A small scratching sound distracted her. The silly-faced balloon was swaying and skittering across the ceiling. Margaret Hall. She didn't remember Kirsten telling her about Margaret before. She scarcely remembered Margaret. I don't remember anything, she thought, glancing up at the snapshot of Billy and Donna and Putter. She scarcely remembered them, either. But she did remember running. Feet flying beneath her, face to the wind. Though Margaret had been fast enough to make the team she had not once, ever, run faster than Janessa. And now? Janessa couldn't run at all. The stupid balloon doing a ballet in the air currents of the room could run faster.

While she still lay there exhausted, Ms. Simpson cheerfulled into the room.

"I've found us some books about Norse mythology," the teacher said, patting a couple of heavy books she carried.

Janessa had forgotten about Ms. Simpson and wished Ms. Simpson had forgotten about her. Eleven o'clock on the dot, Janessa noted as she groaned inwardly. She'd blundered and shown interest the other day and now she was in for it. Ms. Simpson was in green today. Mint and sea.

"I'm sorry these will be too heavy for you to clip to your work board and use yourself," the teacher said.

What a shame, Janessa thought.

"But since I'm not going into this with anyone else, may

I just leave them here to keep from lugging them around?"

Sure, Janessa thought. At least these two thunderous volumes would be out of circulation for a while so no one else would have to be bored by them.

"I've just had an idea," Ms. Simpson said. "I don't know why I didn't think of it. I'll copy some pages and then you can have them in manageable form."

Whoop-de-doo, Janessa thought, but Ms. Simpson's remarks and those ponderous volumes did make Janessa realize she had a question to ask.

"Is there someone named Loki?"

"Just a minute, I'll look in the index." As pleased as lime sherbet punch, Janessa noted, Ms. Mint Simpson searched. "Loki. Yes. Lots about Loki," she said as she kept one finger in the index and looked up appropriate pages. " 'The god Loki was sociable, charming, witty and also cunning, mischievous, and a thief,' " Ms. Simpson read. "And, oh, isn't this interesting! He had certain magic powers including the ability to change his shape. At different times he was in a mare's form, a bird form, he was a fly, a flea, a salmon, a seal. What fun."

Bird form? Janessa saw the falcon fly off with the chartreuse sunglasses. How, she wondered, had her imagination created someone who was already real? Well, mythological. She must have heard about him before.

"Janessa, I can't tell you how delighted I am to be doing this with you. When I was in school, we studied a lot about Greek and Roman mythology, but hardly anything about Norse mythology. I'm embarrassed to say I didn't even know about the days of the week until I started this unit with you." Ms. Simpson was reading on, silently, as though so excited about the Norse gods that she'd forgotten Janessa.

Talk about cunning, Janessa thought. Acting so interested as if to say, Oh, you can't help but be interested in this, Janessa. Fat chance. Too bad Ms. Simpson was wearing green. It wouldn't be distracting enough to name the greens she'd already thought of. Her eye sought out the balloon, which seemed to change corners in the room every time the door opened and closed. I'll count, she thought, and zipped up from 9,930 as Ms. Simpson read on.

"Well, it will take us some time to go over some of this, but there's something I came across while I was reading last night that I thought might interest you."

Ten thousand five, ten thousand six, Janessa said to herself.

"The Rainbow Bridge," Ms. Simpson said.

Janessa stopped, thrown off her guard at 10,007.

These must be stories Dad or Mother told her or read to her when she was little. They had read Greek mythology. She had known Cyclops, with the one big eye, and the flying horse, Pegasus, all her life. Everything Ms. Simpson told her about the Rainbow Bridge and Heimdall, keeper of the bridge, were things she already knew. And more. Ms. Simpson didn't mention how the colors of the bridge rose like mist.

"Well, I just love it," Ms. Simpson said, "but we can't

spend the entire time on Norse mythology. We have science, history, geography, math."

Janessa continued counting from 10,008. When Ms. Simpson left she was on 13,647, and when Mother came ten minutes later she was up to 14,860. It seemed she'd been counting forever and she still wasn't up to twenty thousand. Counting to ten thousand every day, she would need a hundred days to reach a million. She was beginning to realize she might never make it.

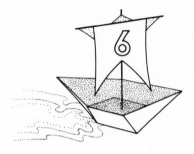

Twice now she had folded a paper ship and, while unfolding it, summoned up the *Skidbladnir*. The first time
was a totally astonishing surprise and the second time, well,
almost a dare. Janessa held a brown sheet of paper almost
afraid to fold it, for this time she was doing it with a wish
and a will. Her planet would be Asgard. She would not be
afraid of the huge gods or back off from her imagination.

Making the creases carefully, she folded and folded and
folded. She plucked at and pulled out the mast, then pulled
the sail from the mast. Then, holding her breath, she pushed

the sail back into the mast, lowered the mast to the body of the ship and began unfolding.

As though hovering, waiting for just this moment, the prow of the huge sailing vessel melded in through glass, steel, and wall. The room lurched to make space.

"Gladden, Janessa. Ready?" Freyr asked, as though no other conversation were necessary. She changed into the tunic and leather breeches and dropped her gown carefully, so it landed on top of herself, the Janessa on the bed. Perhaps this time the two gowns would become one when she returned, the same way the two Janessas became one. If not, she'd at least be able to reach it herself and stuff it somewhere.

"I brought something," he said, and when she looked up from watching the gown float down upon herself he was looking at her cross-eyed.

"My sunglasses!" she said. He took them off and handed them to her.

"You leave here?" Wind was already pulling at the sails.

"No, no," she said, "I want to wear them."

"Then watch for Loki," he said.

Immediately she was sorry she hadn't thought ahead and brought sunglasses for them all, though she didn't know how she would have managed it. What would her parents say if she asked for a half-dozen pairs of sunglasses, large? If Loki had his own sunglasses, he wouldn't have to be snatching hers.

The ship sailed toward a hole in the sky where one perfectly round patch of blue tunneled like a telescope through the deep clouds. As the ship swooshed through, clouds swirled in the draft, then closed up behind them. Above was all bright and sunshiny and below was like heaps of cotton. This time she was interested, excited, pleased and unafraid as the clouds became cloud mountains and ice mountains.

"The river," she said. "The Rainbow Bridge." And there was Heimdall looking down at them, frowning.

"Gladden, Freyr. Her again?"

Everything was comfortably familiar, the colorful mist about Heimdall's ankles, all the green and gold. Now she also saw silver. His un-shadow shining on hill, water, and deck as he came, Goldenbristle leaped to greet them. Loki would be along any moment, she was sure.

This time, she stepped off the ship when Freyr had folded it down to raft size and he continued folding until the ship was tiny and fit the palm of his hand. Opening the pouch fastened to his belt, he slid the ship into it and yanked it closed. Janessa, watching, marveling, was a true believer in this world she had created.

"Can I walk on the Rainbow Bridge?" she asked.

"Aye," Freyr said, "but only halfway." The bridge was so enormous that even halfway would be like counting to a million, she thought.

Heimdall scowled, colors shimmering about his feet and ankles, as he stepped along the bridge toward her.

Fearful, but with Freyr and Goldenbristle at her back, she stepped onto the bridge. The colors puffed up around her feet and legs like dust on a dusty road, and heat rose from the red and yellow stripes.

"Warm!" she said in surprise.

"Aye," Heimdall said. "Melts feet of Frost Giants if they try to cross."

If the giants were bigger than Heimdall, she hoped not to see them, she thought.

"What are those big eyes?" Heimdall asked.

"Oh," she said, touching her face. "Sunglasses." She'd forgotten them. When she took them off to hand to Heimdall, she squinted from the brightness of the Rainbow Bridge.

Heimdall peered through the sunglasses, grunted, and handed them back. "I can't see forever with these big eyes."

A boom of thunder suddenly bounced color sparkles and surrounded Janessa with a kaleidoscope of fog. Heimdall raised his fist and shook it so fiercely she ran down off the bridge.

"This bridge has survived seventeen epochs but will not outlast Thor's idle thunder. He thinks color will last forever," Heimdall growled. "I see the damage. No thing lasts forever."

Ah, Thor. For a moment she'd thought Heimdall's fury was toward her. Safely off the bridge, she looked around, giddy with delight. Silver and gold pathways ran uphill and down. Distant buildings were also made of gold and silver. Huge canopy trees made shade everywhere, but almost everything, except these shadows and trunks of trees, was green. In the pure joy of movement, she stretched out her arms and twirled and twirled until dizziness took her down and it was Asgard that turned. From this angle, an expanse of dark gray-brown caught her eye, like tree bark, but a trunk larger than the live oaks of Hanover, larger than even her imagination could contain. She glanced up and up and up and out and out. In spite of limbs and leaves which umbrellaed everything, the sun shone through.

"Is that a tree?" she asked.

"Aye. Yggdrasil, the World Tree," Freyr said.

"What?" she asked.

"Yggdrasil, the World Tree," he repeated.

"The World Tree," she said, not even trying to pronounce the other word. A fantastic bird dropped from a high limb, spread its wings, and floated down toward them without a wingbeat.

"Loki!" Freyr said.

Janessa was so enchanted with the bird she didn't look around for Loki. The bird drifted soundlessly toward her, encompassing the air, creating its own circle of energy, coming at her, and yet she was not afraid. She firmed her shoulders to her head to brace herself for it to land right on her. Instead, it nipped the sunglasses from her face.

"Loki!" she said, belatedly understanding Freyr's warning. With one strong wingbeat, the bird was back in the tree, chartreuse sunglasses perched on its beak. "Is that bird Loki?"

Freyr nodded, looking wryly amused. The bird looked pretty silly with sunglasses, especially lime-green ones.

"How?" she asked.

"Loki has many shapes," Freyr said.

Ah, yes. Janessa remembered that Ms. Simpson had read about Loki's shapes.

"He has been ant, fly, eel, salmon, horse. Odin's eight-legged steed Sleipnir was Loki's colt."

"Oh," said Janessa, but since Loki's giving or selling a colt to Odin had nothing to do with changing shapes, she knew she'd missed something.

"Loki took horse shape and gave birth to eight-legged colt," Freyr explained.

"Oh," she said again, still watching the bird with the sunglasses. If she reacted too strongly, this wonderful weird movielike dream might stop. A person, even if a Norse god, becomes a bird, becomes a horse and has a colt, and not just a colt but an eight-legged colt. "O-o-okay," she said, and for balance she returned to old information. "What did you say the name of the tree is?"

"Yggdrasil," Freyr said, laughing. "Everything has name. Buildings, weapons, everything. Bridge is Bifrost. Freya's necklace is Brisingamen. Odin's ring is Draupnir, spear is Gungnir. Thor's hammer is Mjolnir."

"Thor," she said, just to stem his flow of names. "Thor's hammer. Yes. That was Thor who made thunder and scattered the colors on the bridge, wasn't it? When do I meet him?"

"Soon," Freyr said. "Odin first."

Odin. Odinsday, Wednesday, she reminded herself. At least she was back with familiar words, Thor and Odin. And this was much more fun than lying dully in the hospital bed! She thought about snapping her fingers to see if this was real, but she was afraid she might snap herself out of Asgard and back into the hospital bed, so she didn't snap. But she pinched herself and it pinched and made a pink mark on her arm. But she was still here, near the Rainbow Bridge, beneath the World Tree, following Freyr through an orchard, which Freyr said was his orchard.

"Look," she said, pointing to the trees as though he hadn't seen them, didn't know them well. She was staring and turning, looking as she stared. There were not various kinds of trees, but various fruits on every tree. A limb of pears, another of apples, another of peaches, and so on for nectarines, oranges, grapefruit, kiwi, guava, and all manner of luscious-looking things she'd never seen before. There were even viny branches of grapes and prickly ones of blackberries and raspberries. All the fruits were outsize, grapes the size of plums and plums the size of apples, but the trees themselves were rather small, though not stunted. She realized at once that the size of the trees gave easy access to the fruit, though she didn't know why that would be necessary when everyone here seemed to have the ability to float or fly.

"I'm a husbandman," Freyr said.

"Oh," she said, thinking how quaint it was to say hus-band-man. Like saying wife-woman, or bow ribbon or movie show or two twins. She nodded, guessing she'd meet his wife later. What was her name, the one with the shining arms? She hoped she could remember every bit of this, to spin and spin and spin from it, and weave it through her dreary days. How odd this was, how magical, as though Freyr, not she, was the one who was making it all up, this fabulous fruit and all those names of things.

On a green hill at the base of a gold tower stood another huge man. She would have called them giants—Freyr, Heimdall, Loki, and this new one with hair falling across one side of his face, covering one eye. On each shoulder was a black bird like a huge crow, and the man frowned down at her from his visible eye.

"Gladden, All-Father," Freyr said to this one who continued to stare at Janessa. "Meet Janessa."

To shake off that one-eyed stare, she dropped her glance and at once jumped back, startled. Beside each of this man's feet was a slack-jawed, drooling wolf. Okay, okay, Janessa, she cautioned herself. You don't have to let your imagination get scary. Heimdall is enough.

"Gladden, Thor. Meet Janessa," Freyr said.

Next to one wolf were two more feet and Janessa raised her eyes up legs and body to see the largest man yet, tall, broad, red-bearded, and holding a hammer. Thor! As if to confirm the identity, Thor pounded the hammer into his own iron-gloved hand. The boom shook the kingdom. The dark birds fluttered up with a croak of protest, then resettled.

"When I foolishly folded myself inside *Skidbladnir*, Janessa is one who unfolded me." The other two men laughed. "Janessa, meet Odin, chief god, All-Father. And meet Thor, god of thunder."

Odin leaned down to shake hands and so did Thor. Odin's was a gentle hand. Thor's was a cruncher.

"Gladden, Janessa," Odin said. "Welcome to Asgard."

"How enter you here?" Thor asked.

It didn't escape her notice that only Freyr and Odin gladdened her to Asgard. "With Freyr," she said. "We came through a hole in the clouds."

"My specialty, clouds," Thor said, and he hurled his hammer toward the distant clouds. Thunder rumbled and lightning flashed along the path of the hammer, and again the enormous crows fluttered and resettled. Janessa looked toward the bridge and watched the mist of color rise and evaporate.

"Cloud making is specialty, not holes in clouds," Odin said as the four of them watched the flight of the hammer.

Thor scowled, and sparks shot out from his bristling red beard.

"Thor's hammer gift from Loki," Freyr said, the hammer disappearing through the clouds, as though it would never return. It left no hole.

"Want wife's hair back," Thor said, shaking an iron-gloved fist. "Want Loki's head."

A third bird, like a falcon or a hawk, appeared from nowhere, but it carried telltale chartreuse sunglasses on its beak. As Janessa's mouth flew open in the surprise of recognition, the bird stretched its claws down to land and became Loki, with the sunglasses perched on his nose.

"My head," Loki said, leaning over, recklessly thrusting his neck out to Thor.

Quickly and almost before thought, Janessa reached out and took the sunglasses from Loki's lowered face. Loki, now with his mouth flown open, raised up and reached out to grab them back, but this time Janessa was not dumb with enchantment. Already she had folded the sidepieces and clutched the sunglasses behind her, out of his casual reach.

Thor roared a huge "Har, har!"

"Aye! Quicker than Loki," Odin said. "You I like, Janessa."

"What are those?" Thor asked.

"Sunglasses," she said, holding them away from Loki but toward Thor. Thor held them to his eyes and tilted his head back as he peered through them, saying, "Hmmm." Then he passed them to Odin, who did the same, and who handed them back to Janessa. Loki was watching like the eagle which he'd become, and, wings extended, he leaped and landed heavily on Janessa's head. The talons dug in like Crutchfield tongs.

"Hold still," Freyr said quickly. "Do not let him snatch sunglasses."

She hunched her shoulders to shrink her head into her body, for strength, but she did not move the sunglasses from their secure position.

"Where you get such gift?" Odin asked. His tone was stern, almost unfriendly, and this just after he said he liked her. "You been to Elves of Ivaldi?"

"Nay, All-Father," Freyr said, answering for her. "Janessa bring big eyes from Midgard. Loki stole, as he steals everything he get hands, beak, claws on."

Followed by rumbling thunder, the hammer came twirling back from the clouds. In one motion, Thor reached out for it and swung at Janessa's head. Rather, at the eagle upon it, but the effect was the same. Janessa ducked and Loki took human shape, but small, smaller than Janessa. He shrank behind her and Thor looked ready to smash Janessa to get at Loki.

"Thor!" Odin roared, shaking his head forcefully. Hair fell away from the covered eye, and there was no eye. Just the top and bottom eyelids caved in upon an empty socket.

Janessa shuddered, and shook her head to clear the fantasy, but it stuck like spider silk. Her feet were still on Asgard ground. She was here with three enormous men, a fourth who changed sizes and shapes at will, two giant crows, two wolves, and a huge gold boar that frolicked as though it were a small brown dog like Putter.

Something tugged at her hand. It was Loki, still small in size, tugging at the sunglasses, but she had them so firmly gripped he didn't get them. Bending her elbow, she raised her hand and clasped the glasses against her chest.

Odin laughed at Loki and at Janessa's strong hold on the sunglasses. "I also have gift from Loki. For his mischief we find no cure, and he is always before the council. He redeems himself with gifts from Elves of Ivaldi." Odin held out his hand and showed her his ring. "As symbol of welcome and sign of my protection in Asgard, please wear my ring."

His ring? It had, she saw, a single eye at the center. A one-eyed ring from the one-eyed god. But it would be so large, she would have to worry constantly about losing it.

The ring even increased in size, bulging as if turning soft and swelling like bread dough, and as she watched, a second ring formed from the first. Odin took this one and slid it onto her middle finger where it diminished to fit her.

"You are under my eye," he said, looking at her two eyes with his one. "Go about kingdom with my protection."

"Protection?" she asked. Wasn't this a gold and silver kingdom? From what would she need protection? She wanted to be safe because the world was safe, not because she was protected and there were things to be protected from.

"Think!" squawked one of the crows.

"Remember!" squawked the other.

Odin still held out his hand. The ring was still reproducing. "Watch," he said. "Every nine days, eight more rings." The rings chimed against each other as he caught them in his hand. Reaching behind him, he put the new rings in a gold box with dozens of others. The box itself had a border design of rings. Other rings formed decorations on the gold tower.

Amidst the multiplying of the rings was another Asgard wonder. A multicolored hummingbird shimmered about her, wings whirring thousands of beats a minute. The hummingbird looked as though it had flown through the mist of the Rainbow Bridge, red, yellow, blue, green, like the birds, painted buntings, in Hanover.

"Janessa," Freyr said.

Too late she heard the warning in his tone and at the

moment when she was most mesmerized, the delicate whirring bird hooked the hinge of the sunglasses with its needle beak and sped away.

"Loki!" they all said, but she was laughing as they said it, laughing at the charm and cleverness of it. As soon as they saw she was laughing, they laughed, too, and shook their heads. Then she realized she was laughing.

Laughing!

She hadn't laughed since the outrage. It felt better to laugh, even, than to move her head or run. She looked at them, Freyr, Odin, Thor, to see if they knew what wonderful thing had happened to her, but she saw they didn't. They didn't know her, didn't know there was anything unusual in this laughter. She would have given a dozen pairs of sunglasses for this laughter. Loki could have them all. She broke from the group and ran racing and laughing toward the orchard.

W ith the wind singing in her ears she ran free, slinging an arm about first this tree, then that, whirling herself around before running on. The bark of these trees was as smooth as velvet and there was every kind of fruit, plump on the branches. Here is where she would live forever, not in the stupid hospital room. Here is where she could run free and not be in danger. Her family could come live with her here. And Lynn.

Lynn. She'd shut Lynn out. Lynn, her best friend. Lynn who'd sent a note or card every single day since she'd been hurt. Lynn who had wanted to come see her and she had said no and no and no. They didn't understand how seeing anyone made her hurt for them simply because they were in the world where there were avalanches and airplane crashes and automobile accidents and girls grabbed from the doorways of neighborhood stores. And Lynn, her running mate, could still run.

But here Janessa could run, too. How perfect it would be to have Lynn here, to run and laugh with. To show her the Rainbow Bridge and how the colors bounced when Thor made thunder. To show her the *Skidbladnir* and the way it folded down to fit the pouch. And let her see the painted hummingbird which could steal sunglasses many times its own weight and still fly with a whiz of grace.

The giant-sized fruit on the trees pulsed with ripeness. The apples, pears, and peaches were too large for her to sink her teeth into, but she picked some plum-sized grapes that were sweet and seedless. She stretched out her hand to the sun and examined the glint of Odin's ring. There was a pair of birds on one side. Those crows, she guessed. And on the other side was a pair of wolves. An arrow followed the curve of the ring from the birds to the wolves. Or was it a spear? Hadn't Freyr said something about a spear? Rather, hadn't she thought something about a spear? This was her fantasy, she reminded herself, then wished she hadn't. Would remembering this was a fantasy make it disappear, like waking from a dream you wanted to finish but seldom could?

To stay in the dream, she began whirling again, laughing,

stretching, whirling so fast that wind hummed in her ears. Then another sound mixed with the humming of the wind. She stopped to listen and was charmed to hear laughter and singing in the distance. Twirling again, she lost herself in the rhythm and beat of the music and the laughter until she was deep inside herself, or lost in this space of Asgard, laughing and spinning until she tripped over something. She and the grapes fell splashing into a silver stream.

The water smelled like honeysuckle. Scooping a handful, she sniffed. Hmmm, yes, honeysuckle. She slurped from her hand and the water tasted cool and sweet, but not like honeysuckle. The water was cold to drink, yet she wasn't cold from falling in. The grapes stared up from the bottom like purple eyes.

"There are more grapes, Janessa," someone said.

Startled, Janessa looked up and saw a huge woman whose glow lit up the already sunny air. A goddess? At the same instant, she realized she had tripped over this goddess on her Tilt-A-Whirl run. Floundering to right herself, she sputtered, "Oh, I'm sorry, I'm sorry."

"Quite all right, Janessa. Gladden. Good to see you enjoying Asgard."

"I—I—you know me? Who are you?" Janessa asked, and immediately she knew. "You're Gerd!"

"Nay. Gerd has shining arms, not shining hair." The woman ran her hand along her neck beneath the gold hair and flipped it so that it caught the sunlight and scattered gold dust the way the Rainbow Bridge sprayed colors. "I am Sif, wife of Thor."

"Oh," Janessa said, trying to remember what she'd heard about Thor's wife.

"Thor brought me big eyes," Sif said, holding out the sunglasses. "They're yours, I believe."

"Oh, no," Janessa said. "You keep them. I'd like you to have them." On the goddess with gold hair the chartreuse sunglasses didn't look one bit silly.

"Thor told me about your hair. About Loki cutting it. I'm sorry. At least I guess I'm sorry. I know you wish it hadn't happened, but your hair now . . ." She was babbling, mesmerized by this hair, hair like Goldenbristle's.

"Aye," she said, stroking and flipping the hair again. "Thor would. Would he give back hammer for my other hair? I like gold hair," she said, tugging at it. "Is real hair. It grows. Who but me has gold hair? Would I give it back?"

"I wouldn't," Janessa said, shaking her head so her hair swung, wishing it scattered gold dust. How could she bait Loki into cutting her hair and replacing it with spun gold? With a glance at Odin's ring she dismissed the idea. The ring, she supposed, would protect her from any such mischief as hair cutting, even if she wished it.

"What is that singing?" she asked, settled enough from her encounter with Sif to hear the music and laughter again.

"Valkyries coming to Valhalla," Sif said, smiling, and her smile lit her face as though her mouth, too, were made of gold.

"May I go see?"

"Aye, aye," Sif said. "Grace be with you."

"Will you come with me?" Janessa asked.

"Nay, gladden. I must watch for Grundor to bring fish eggs."

"Aye," Janessa said. Caviar, even here? "Gladden," she said, pleased to use their form of language. "Grace be with you."

The new laughter bubbled again as she ran off toward the music, the harmonic rhythm pulling her as though it were the Pied Piper. As she ran and leaped and twirled over a knoll from the orchard, she saw a surge of people coming down from the Rainbow Bridge. A parade? Long lines of them marched toward a building which seemed to be all doors. A party? Who were the Valkyries? The people were not in lines, really, but in groups, like children leaving school, except these weren't children. They were smaller than Freyr, Heimdall, Odin, Thor, Loki, but larger than her father. Their singing was fierce but joyful. Triumphant. She liked the energetic sound of it. The confidence.

Looking behind to check her bearings, the orchard was out of sight. Had she come too far? Shrugging, she moved forward again, toward the parade, no longer running but moving closer, stopping, moving closer. With a start she realized it was a costume party. One of the men was dressed with his collar over his head and was carrying a head. She shivered, and was surprised at that because she liked horrid monster costumes for Halloween whereas Lynn always dressed as Snow White or Peter Pan or something equally bland and unHalloweenish. Did they have Halloween in Asgard? Is that what this was? What a wonderful idea for a costume! She was stopped for the moment, looking at that one, thinking of exactly how you'd concoct such a costume and look out through the front of your clothes. But how would you make such a realistic looking head? Papier-mâché? She always made such a mess with papier-mâché. This man's head even had blood dripping from it. She shivered again. Blood dripped from the arm holding the head. Even when she dressed as a vampire with lipstick as blood dripping from her mouth, which had frightened Billy and Donna, she hadn't been this repulsive. She looked away.

Another man was hopping along on one leg, while appearing to carry the other. Gruesome! How had they thought of these things? She inched closer. Where was his second leg, so skillfully tucked up beneath his clothing? The fake leg he carried was dripping blood and had the bone sticking out.

Only the men were in costume, she noticed, and all with ghastly, deadly looking wounds. If they had head and limbs attached, they were run through or sliced open. One had an eyeball—a grape?—hanging halfway down his cheek and he was singing, singing lustily and with merriment. The women, splendid, ghostlike, in thin, flowing, colorful cloth, were helping the men along, even carrying some of them.

As she watched, her open mouth got dry and a sourness cramped her stomach. This was too real. The men were pale but not at all ghostlike and the song, the haunting song, was like a death song, a joyous and triumphant death song. And, yes, she had not mistaken it, they were laughing.

And then she saw the pair of crows and the pair of wolves darting along, nipping, ripping at flesh, as though having supper. One crow snapped off the dangling eyeball! There was the feel of a huge thorn in her throat, both compelling her to scream and cutting off the scream. This was not real, these hundreds in this hideous blood procession. She was making this up. But why? Why? She didn't want to see any hurt thing ever again.

To prove to herself she was imagining, she ran forward into the group, into the parade, making herself laugh and take up their song. And, reaching out, she touched a man who was carrying his arm.

He was there.

Solid.

At her touch, he jumped in surprise and dropped his arm which fell against her and she jerked back, blood all over her, and the thorn feeling ripped out of her throat with a scream as she ran again, running, running, yelling with the smell of blood in her nostrils and no more laughter in her.

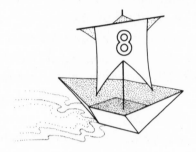

Freyr found her. She was cowering in a heap at the raised root of a tree, her hands over her ears to shut out the unending drone of laughing and singing.

"What happened?" he asked, gently removing her hands from her ears.

She shook her head, yanked her hands loose, and covered her ears again. How many were there? Wouldn't they ever go inside that building and shut all those doors?

Again, he took her hands away from her ears. "Heimdall heard you," he said.

Heimdall, she thought, who could see to the ends of the world, who could hear fruit growing. Heimdall who seemed so gruff. "Those people," she said.

He watched her hands go back over her ears, tilted his head to hear what she was blocking out. "Yes, what about them?" This time he'd just moved one of her hands and only a few inches.

"They're dead," she said.

"Yes," he said pleasantly. "Dead being brought to Valhalla."

"But if they're dead," she said, "how can they be—be alive?"

"Oh, they're quite dead," he said. "Will not be alive again until morning, after night of feasting and celebrating."

"But they're singing," she said. "And laughing."

"Of course," he said. "Have died boldly in battle, and laughed at deathblow. To them is highest honor, to celebrate in Odin's hall."

The gall burned Janessa's throat and she struggled to keep from vomiting. She would never have made it to Odin's hall. If she had died in the fall from that car, she would not have died in laughter but in terror. Who would want to join such a dreadful procession?

"What kind of place is this?" she asked.

"What kind of place did you think?"

She looked at him sharply, to see if he'd turned into Dr. Gilder, answering a question with a question. He was still Freyr, large and blond and bearded.

"Safe," she said. "I thought it was safe."

In sudden alarm, he asked, "Did someone harm you?"

"Ye-esss!" she wailed. She felt harmed. "No-o-o," she cried. She wasn't physically harmed, not like being shoved out of a moving car. She shook her finger toward the distant guttural sounds. "I'm supposed to be under Odin's protection."

"My lass," he said, kindly. "In every world, in every time, there is hazard. War, wolves, weather." He was looking at her in puzzlement. "Even with the protection of the gods, no place is entirely safe. I thought you knew that. But the brave can live well anywhere."

Words were worthless, she thought, yanking Odin's ring off her finger and flinging it.

Freyr lunged to catch it.

But another hand was there, catching it. Odin.

Freyr and Odin looked at each other and shrugged.

"Get her away from here," the All-Father said, with a wave of his hand.

Without even waiting to walk to the river, Freyr opened the pouch, removed its contents, and flapped them to the air. The *Skidbladnir* unfurled, gunnels, deck, sails, and all. Freyr boosted Janessa aboard and they were off in a huff, as if the North Wind had emptied its entire breath into the sails.

The last things she remembered before her parents' voices woke her were the venetian blinds banging and the balloon careening around the ceiling. Had she slept or only gotten lost up there against the ceiling? She sidled her eyes to see them coming, both of them together.

"Well, you don't have to look so grim-lipped," her mother said, and her heart jumped when she realized they weren't yet in the room, that the voice, dim, was coming through the door from the hall. They were talking about her. What was making them grim-lipped? She would never run again. Never walk! How many days had she lain here, ears stretched, trying to catch information from the hall, hearing nothing. And now, now, she didn't want to hear it. Still, she held her breath, to stop the pounding of her heart, trying to hear more. Their voices were intense, sounding almost like a quarrel, but she could only catch the tone, not the words.

The air "whoomphed" at the opening of the door and the balloon scraped and scurried across the ceiling. Janessa swallowed as her parents came in, tense against their being sticky sweet or telling her anything she didn't want to hear.

Dad was in a short-sleeved sport shirt instead of his usual business suit.

"Is this Saturday?" she asked, knowing it wasn't, but feeling so out of kilter.

"Nah," Dad said, acknowledging his Saturday clothes with a lift of elbows, raising his thoroughly freckled arms to the air. "A holiday." He set the cello down by the bedside table as both parents came to kiss and cuddle. Her gown was dry. She was no longer sweaty and chilly. Now she was hot with knowing, with not wanting to know.

"Did you learn the Mozart Quartett?"

"Yes," he said. "I'll play it for you in a little while."

Usually he was so pleased when he learned a new piece, but he didn't seem entirely happy. Both of them seemed hot, also, and trying to pretend good spirits against grim lips. What was the bad news about her? The dinner tray came and Dad tended to settling it across her while Mother busied herself about the drawers and closet. The air was so prickly, Janessa found it difficult to chew and swallow.

"Come on, baby," Dad said. "If you don't eat, your stomach will be growling all night and keep the rabbits awake." Origami rabbits still populated the room, but Dad's jokes could not unlock the fear.

Putting some clean things in a drawer, Mother looked up with eyebrows drawn down and close together. In one hand, she held a freshly laundered yellow gown and in the other, the rumpled one from the bottom of the drawer. "I didn't realize Mother had made two yellow gowns," she said aloud, more musing to herself than to Dad or Janessa. "I thought she'd made each one different."

"Perhaps you've been distracted," Dad said with an edge to his voice that felt like a pinch to Janessa.

Of course they'd been distracted, Janessa was thinking, when her mother huffed, actually huffed.

"Your father is upset about my new account," Mother said.

"Whyyy?" Janessa said, pouncing on it, relieved to have any subject in this room except the one she dreaded, the one that caused grim lips in the hall.

Mother shrugged. "He considers it competition."

"Why? What kind of account is it?" Competition was trying to win against someone else. Janessa couldn't imagine Mother doing anything against Daddy.

"You through?" Daddy said to her, and cleared away the tray.

"The Atlantic Coastal Bank," Mother said.

"Ohhh," Janessa said, understanding a little, but not much. Atlantic Coastal was the other bank, the one Daddy didn't work for. "Then why don't you get the account at Daddy's bank?"

Daddy looked exasperated and Mother looked victorious. If there was victory, then maybe there was competition, Janessa thought. Daddy unzipped the canvas case of the cello, hooked his foot under the rung of a nearby chair, and dragged it to him.

"Whyyy?" Janessa said again, doing the opposite of what she did with Ms. Simpson. Instead of trying to ignore them into silence, she tried to keep them going.

"Do we have to have these complications?" Daddy asked. He sat, straddling the instrument, and bowed and tuned, bowed and tuned.

"Yes," Janessa said quickly. She wanted to stop this evasiveness between her parents. What terrible thing was wrong with her? Or was it really between them and nothing to do with her at all? Her feelings rose and sank. It would be good, wouldn't it, if she was going to get well like they said? But she wanted every word between them to be about her.

"Are you ready for the Mozart Quartett?" Daddy asked and, without waiting for the response, began the murmur of bow across strings, his one part of four.

Suddenly she did not want to hear him play. His arms, loose from the long shirt and suit sleeves that usually covered them, were too bare, too raw, too free. What was he doing in short sleeves if it wasn't even Saturday? What were they doing, getting into an argument here in her hospital room? The light glistened off the red-gold hair on his arms and suddenly she wanted him to leave, wanted them to leave. She tried to hold it, contain it as the cello began coursing out the Mozart, listening for the thirty-second notes that were so difficult. But the bow against the strings sounded so much like moaning, like her moaning when they'd come to do the X-ray, when Kirsten came to do the therapy, when she saw the bloody parade in Valhalla, when she first heard their near-quarreling voices in the hall and she was afraid.

"Can you bring me six pairs of sunglasses?" she said abruptly, not looking at them, but staring up. Mother said, "What?" and Dad kept on playing, uninterruptible once he began, and there was that dumb, pink happy-faced balloon bobbing to the music as though it were alive and dancing. She had meant to ask for the sunglasses with the utmost charm and persuasion and here she was blurting, demanding in a frantic high-pitched voice. "As big and funky as you can find. They're for joke gifts and I have to have them," she said, trying to roll over her father's cello playing, and suddenly, as though she were a balloon, she popped.

"I want you to go," she said. "I want you both to go."

After all this wanting them to come, wanting them to stay, she couldn't have shocked them more.

"What is it, sweetheart?" Dad said, startled into stopping. Bow in hand, he came to her, they both came to her.

"I'll bring the sunglasses, Janny," Mother said, stroking her head. "Who knows what you want them for, but I'll bring them."

She wanted to pull away, wanted to say, "Don't touch me," but she couldn't pull away and words seemed so useless. They touched her, arms, head, sides of face, touches that she loved and craved until this moment. Now their hands and fingers seemed to burn wherever they touched.

"Now," she said as fiercely as she'd said it to Freyr to get home from Asgard. "I want you to leave now."

Daddy looked alarmed but ready to leave, ready to comply with anything she wished, but Mother held out a cautioning "wait-a-minute" hand to him. "We'll just sit for a few minutes until you can calm down and tell us what's wrong," Mother said.

"I don't want to tell anybody anything," Janessa said, just short of shouting. "I don't know what's wrong." They sat, pulling the chairs to the far wall, and the only way she could close them out was to close her eyes. She pressed fingertips to her mouth as if to hold something in. What? What? What was happening to her?

"Yes?" came a voice over the intercom.

"We need a nurse," Mother said, "and perhaps a sedative."

Mother must have pressed the nurse-call button when she was near the bed. Whisper-foot came in as though she'd been ready and waiting for the call. She glanced at Mother and Daddy but came to Janessa. "What is it? What's happened to upset you?"

How did the nurse know she was upset? She'd removed her hand from her mouth and was just lying here like her normal immobile self. She stared at the stupid happy-faced balloon that had fairly bounced across the ceiling in the draft of the opening door. She said nothing.

"The bedpan, too, I guess," Mother said.

She wanted to say no, no bedpan, no more bedpan. What made them think she needed the bedpan? And what did she care if she wet the bed? If she held it and held it and held it perhaps she would be able to pee enough to float herself away from here.

To where? To where?

Grabbing for her work tray, she looked at the last number she'd written down, 14,860. "Fourteen thousand eight hundred sixty-one," she said loudly. "Fourteen thousand eight hundred sixty-two. Fourteen thousand eight hundred sixty-three." She hurled numbers into the room, her parents sitting over against the wall as though pinned there by numbers, the nurse touching her hair and saying, "There, there." In her fury, she thought surely she could reach a million by midnight. But at 15,745 she couldn't say one more number.

All night, the number 15,745 spun in her head, wove itself into fabric, stitched itself onto quilts, printed itself onto her two yellow gowns. The number wrapped around her father's freckled arms and became the cello bow and turned into musical notes which rose to the ceiling and chased the dumb balloon around the room. In the morning, as though it had also had a bad night, the balloon sagged a foot below the ceiling with no more scrape, scrape, scrape across the ceiling.

In the midst of the morning hustle and bustle—breakfast, morning washup, temperature, pulse and blood pressure taken, the orthopedic doctor checking out her bones—Mother came, crossing to the bed for huggles and snuggles just like always.

"She's a quiet one this morning," the nurse said to Mother.

"You okay, baby?" Mother asked, then. "Are you all right?"

Janessa wanted to answer yes, to let everything be all right, but she was mute, not just in voice, but in brain. No words even came to her. Something was terribly wrong, but she had no idea what.

When she was silent and still for a moment too long, Mother said, "Janny, baby, what is it? What's going on? You have to tell me, sweetheart."

She couldn't even manage one of her feeble shrugs, just lay there stiff and staring at the ceiling, watching the balloon waggle about in the moving air of the room. Mother hovered and probed until Janessa pressed her lips together to keep from shouting at her to go away. Mother paced and fussed about the room, straightening the already straight drawer, aligning hangers in the closet.

Don't you have to go to work? Janessa thought, through gritted brain and gritted teeth, but she didn't part her lips to let the words pass.

Mother was near the door when Dr. Gilder came scurrying in. They made a graceful dodge in the entry space as Dr. Gilder shut the door behind him.

"Ah, Dr. Gilder," said Janessa's mother, and now Janessa knew why Mother had been hanging around.

"Oh, Mrs. Kessel," said Dr. Gilder, slowing, stopping, extending a hand. "Good morning, Mrs. Kessel. Good morning, Janessa." He came directly to Janessa, and gave her the total-paying-attention sort of look that he always gave.

"May I see you for a minute, Dr. Gilder?" Janessa's mother said, following him to the bedside, as though he might not hear from the doorway.

Janessa's spirits flattened out along her spine. They were going to talk. About her. About her condition, about her behavior. They were going to dissect her and set out her body parts right here in front of her without benefit of anesthesia. She grimaced and closed her eyes, which was the only defense she had.

Of course they talked about her, she knew that, but they never gave any suggestion of it, had never even whispered outside her door, until last night.

"Not now, if you don't mind, Mrs. Kessel. This is my time with Janessa." He moved away from Mother, away from the bedside and stepped to the window, adjusting the blind so the morning sun was full in Janessa's face.

"But this is about Janessa," Mother said. "It's important."

Dr. Gilder took the horizontal output tube from his pocket and held it between thumb and forefinger to show Janessa. "If you'll excuse me," he said. "I assumed it was about Janessa, and I assume it is important." He gave the tube a very small toss. "May I call you later? At your office?" With his quick movements, he returned to the door he'd just closed and he opened it, a direct invitation for Mother to leave. Mother looked sideways at both of them, but moved on out, through the doorway and into the hall, and Dr. Gilder closed the door behind her.

Janessa bit her lip at the rudeness. The satisfying and embarrassing rudeness. But hadn't Mother been rude to start to talk to Dr. Gilder right in front of her?

Coming back across the room, before he'd even reached the end of the bed or picked up the clipboard with her chart, Dr. Gilder said, "What's this about a sedative last night?"

So, he knew, anyway, without Mother telling.

In her first words of the morning and in her most withering tone, she said, "My mother." And then after what she considered a significant pause, she announced, "I've counted to 15,745."

"I'm impressed," he said.

"If I count to ten thousand every day, it will take me one hundred days to count to a million," she said.

"I'm even more impressed. That you could figure that out."

"It just takes dividing. It was easy," she said. "A million is a lot."

"It is, indeed," he said. "Don't you want your sunglasses?"

"I don't have them," she said. She decided she might as well not make a pretense of looking for them.

"What happened to them?" he asked, moving over, taking his own from his pocket and sliding them onto her face.

"Someone took them," she said, and by the surprised and saddened look on his face she knew she'd said the wrong thing.

"No, I mean, they must be around here somewhere," she said quickly, fumbling through her tray. He would think someone here took them, someone at the hospital. He looked on the bed, under the bed, and then asked, "May I?" for permission to look through the dresser and in the closet. "Sure," she said. What did she know? They might be here somewhere. The gown she'd tossed in imagination had been here in reality, so perhaps the sunglasses Loki stole and Thor gave to Sif would be here, too.

She remembered her wish to pee enough so she floated herself to freedom. "I wish," she said, "I could find someplace between here and there. Where there is no danger, no fear."

"Between here and where?" he asked, holding out his hands to show he had not found the sunglasses.

Always answering a question with a question. She hated that. She meant between here and Asgard, but she assumed he'd think between here and home. "Between here," she said, "and there."

"Or maybe here," she added. "If I could live in this room forever."

"What we have to do, then, is to figure out how you can have the life you want here in this room."

His words swirled and lurched and comforted, but she

didn't understand what he meant. How could she have the life she wanted in this room?

"What do you mean?" she asked, almost in a whisper.

"First we have to talk about what kind of life you want."

Not only had she not thought about it, she had been actively not thinking about it. "Asgard," she said, though that wasn't really the answer. She wanted only a part of Asgard, the first part, the Asgard of the Rainbow Bridge, the gold rings, the giant fruit, and even the charming, mischievous Loki. Everything she saw before the bloody parade of the dead. But she didn't know if she really wanted a fantasy world forever. She didn't know where she wanted to be forever except, maybe, in this room.

"Asgard?" he questioned.

"The Norse gods."

"Oh," he said, nodding. "They're a pretty rough bunch, aren't they?"

Yes, she thought. I guess they are.

"Not to me," she said.

"Okay," he said. "We can paint the Rainbow Bridge across that wall and Thor can throw his lightning bolts from this window. And that's the extent of my knowledge of the Norse gods."

"Tuesday, Wednesday, Thursday, Friday," she said. When he looked puzzled, she explained about the days of the week. "And Thor doesn't throw lightning bolts, he makes thunder," she continued. "Everyone has it backwards about lightning and thunder. Thor hammers to make thunder, and the hammering sets off sparks which is the lightning, but it's the thunder first and then the lightning."

"I see," he said, nodding again. "And since light is faster than sound, we see the lightning before we hear the thunder."

"Mmm," she said in surprise. She hadn't thought of that. "Yes," she said. "Maybe so." The speed of light reminded her of her own speed, running through the neighborhood, around the school yard, down a track, along the deck of the *Skidbladnir,* and through the orchards of Asgard.

"I want to be a runner," she said.

Dr. Gilder didn't blink, didn't look thoughtful or puzzled, but made the leap from Norse gods, thunder and lightning. "If we moved the bed to the center of the room and shoved the chairs and tables to the entryway," he said, arms and hands indicating the moves, "you could have a practice track for when you're mobile again."

"Oh, sure," she said. "A whole new way of racing, a small square instead of a large oval or a straightaway."

"Why not?" he said. "It's your life. You're entitled to make some choices. You get to make some of the rules."

"Can we try it? Making the track?"

"Why not?" he said, and began shoving chairs, bedside table, dresser, television, and her two work trays into the entry alcove, then carried the plants, flowers, basket of cards and perched them on top of, in, and under. Saying "Oof," he tugged and shoved her bed to the center of the room. "Okay, where's the starting line?"

She shrugged her little shrug.

"You say," he said. "It's your rules."

She pointed to the tumble of furniture in the alcove and he stepped to that part of the room and crouched, one hand to the floor.

"Ready. Set. Go!" she said.

Sprinting to the first corner, he skidded along the wall to the second, bounced off with his foot to turn toward the third corner, and whipped back along the fourth wall to the entry and stopped.

"Laps," she said. "There will have to be a lot of laps."

He took off again and made three circuits before he stopped.

"We'll need a stopwatch."

He snapped his fingers. "I knew we forgot something." He looked at his watch, announced the position of the second hand, and sped around one more time. "Five and a half split seconds," he said. "If you practice the timing of your steps you can get that left leg out for more efficient turns."

"No feet on the walls," she said, pointing to where his shoe had made a smudge at each contact point.

"Oops," he said, stooping, rubbing the wall, but his rubbing only smudged the smudge. He made a face. "Good rule, no feet on the walls. Wish you'd told me that one before. Any other rules?"

"I make the rule that nobody ever robs stores," she said.

"That's a good rule."

"I make the rule that no one ever grabs someone and drags them off."

Dr. Gilder nodded.

"And slams them out of a car onto moving pavement." For that's how it had seemed to her, that the car was stationary and the road was whizzing along beneath her. There was horror from the road, horror from the car, and she had no safe place to go, in the car or out, and she'd had to cling to the arm of this person she wanted to get away from.

"The corners would sure slow me down," she said, returning to racing to keep herself from slamming into that pavement one more time.

"I don't know how you kept from dropping dead of terror," he said.

"I guess I could learn to use my hands at the corners, and make those turns the way a swimmer does in a pool. It'll be my track," she said. "I guess I can make the rules. I wonder what timing a good lap would be?"

In a very quiet voice, he said, "Oh, about five and a half seconds, when you get as good as me."

All she could hear was the loud swishing sound of the moving pavement as he tried to dislodge her and push her out. All she could see was his pale face, blond hair as he pried her fingers loose from his arm. She suddenly loved Dr. Gilder for having nothing blond about him, and she was as hot and sweaty as though she'd had the X-ray plates shunted beneath her again. Or had run twenty laps around the room, bouncing off walls to make the corners.

"Arms," she said.

"Yes," he said. "It would depend on perfecting the arm work at the corners."

Something was lodging there in her throat, blocking her air passage, not wanting to go up or down, and she didn't know whether to swallow or throw up. There was something she wanted to tell Dr. Gilder but the idea of it wouldn't quite form into words, and the need to tell what she couldn't think of started her crying and she sniffed to stop crying and couldn't stop so she kept crying and sniffing.

"It's all right to cry, Janessa," Dr. Gilder said.

So she quit sniffing and cried outright, bawling and bellowing one minute and mewing like a sick kitten the next. When she was finally slowing down, Dr. Gilder dampened a washcloth with warm water and wiped her face, removed the sunglasses, and put them in her hand.

In a minute or two, very softly, he asked, "Can you tell me what that was about? Anything at all?"

Just the question set off her crying again, but briefly this time.

"Anything?"

With lips quivering and pressed together she shook her head, meant to shake her head, wanted to shake her head and once again she came butt up against the fact that it would not shake, and she shouted, "Damn it!"

"Good girl!" Dr. Gilder said, punching his fist into his other hand. "Say it again."

"Damn it!"

"Again."

"DAMN IT!"

"Again."

If the walls had been papered, that next one would have been a paper peeler. But the ones after diminished until the last one was a whimper.

"You've worked *hard*," he said, touching her cheek in the same tender way as Dad. For a while they just remained quiet, then he said, "Listen, I'll be in the hospital until one o'clock this afternoon and if you want me, I can be here in two minutes, okay? After that, I'll be in my office and I can be here in ten minutes."

"You'd do that?" she asked, remembering her disappointment when she'd realized she wasn't his only patient.

"Of course," he said.

Of course, she thought. No matter how many other people he took care of, he was her Dr. Gilder. He was her Dr. Gilder pulling, pushing, shoving furniture back into place, trying to hide the smudges. She could call him anytime, if she wanted, and he would come. When he left, he forgot his sunglasses. She put them back on, these cool dude shades, to cover her puffy eyes.

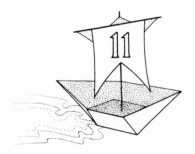

Who she wanted first, strangely enough, was Ms. Sunshine Simpson. She had a zillion questions she wanted to ask about Valkyries and Valhalla. Anything to keep from wondering why she was so upset with her parents last night.

The book. Ms. Scarlet Simpson had left the book. She could find out things for herself. She touched the call button at the side of the bed and the invisible monitoring nurse said, "Yes? What can we do for you, Janessa?" Until now, she had never called for anything except medical, bodily, or closing-window help, and she felt stupid now asking them to fetch a book. Most of her things were in reach in her work tray. The words "I want someone to hand me a book" just wouldn't get past a stuck place in her throat.

"Janessa? Are you all right, Janessa?" the unseen nurse asked. And swiftly, before Janessa could get her tongue moving, a nurse bustled in.

"You okay?" A quick touch of the head, check of the pulse. "You look okay."

"I wanted someone to hand me a book," she said, waving her arm. "That one under the table. The one on mythology."

"This one?" the nurse said in surprise, stooping, lifting. "Now what in the world do you think you're going to do with this?" The woman hoisted the book and held it out to Janessa. "I don't believe your book clip can handle it, do you?"

"Oh," Janessa said. She had paid so little attention to Ms. Fuchsia Simpson she didn't realize the book was like three volumes of the *Encyclopedia Britannica* put together. "I don't guess I can manage that," she said.

"No, I don't suppose you can," said the nurse. "Want me to see if I can get you a reader? We have people who volunteer to come read to patients."

"No," Janessa said, feeling alarmed at the idea of some stranger coming into her room. "I'll just wait until Mom and Daddy come, I guess."

"You sure? You get mighty bored in here, I know. Don't you? Did you get your TV fixed yet?"

Janessa felt her head nodding, nodding, shaking, knowing it wasn't really moving and not knowing which question to answer.

"No reader. I'm sure," she said.

"Okay, then, if you're sure," the nurse said, reaching out to fluff the pillow under her good leg, straightening the already straight sheet.

What she'd do, she decided, is think about what questions she wanted answered. Could someone tell her about Valhalla and the Valkyries in some sort of bloodless way? Shuddering from the memory of that arm falling against her, she decided to continue her count to a million instead of thinking up questions. She scrabbled on the top of her side table until she found the piece of paper where she'd written down her last number: 15,745. How could she forget it when she'd dreamed of it all night long? Zipping along with these numbers wasn't so easy, now that they were so large, and it took immense concentration to keep track.

Somewhere along in the eighteen thousand one hundred seventies, feeling twenty thousand straight ahead, she yawned, on the verge of closing her eyes and dropping off to sleep. She closed her eyes but said a few more numbers to get to one she could remember, because she didn't even have the energy to reach for the pencil and paper: 18,188. She could remember all those eights. And she dozed off with eights floating in the air like the silly-faced balloon.

She awoke with a jolt. Someone had come into the room. She looked, and there was Daddy, sitting quietly and quite settled by the bed as though he'd been there awhile. "My number, my number," she said, closing her eyes again, trying to see the number. Where had she left off?

"How are you, baby?" he said.

"My number!" she said with irritation, screwing up her face to shut him out, to shut out "baby." The number where she stopped was all the same number. Which number? Ah, yes, threes. She opened her eyes, reached for paper and pencil and held them above her and wrote 88,888. For one moment she was so elated it almost took her breath then she realized, no, she'd been close to twenty thousand, had gotten into twenty thousand. She crossed out the number and wrote 28,188. Now she was approaching thirty thousand. "I'm counting to a million," she told her father.

"A million. I'm impressed. How far have you gotten?"
She told him.

He pursed his lips and nodded. "That's quite a lot. I don't think I ever counted that high in my life. Ready for dinner?"

"It's here?"

"They're bringing it. You can hear the carts chugalugging down the hall." At just that minute, a rose-dressed aide brought in the tray. Janessa decided her favorite colors were going to be gray and black.

"Afterwards, would you read to me?" she asked.

"Of course," he said, setting the tray on the bedside table and sliding the table across her, swinging the mirror over it so she could look up to see down.

"What is that? Beets?" she said, wrinkling her nose. "I didn't ask for beets."

"What did you ask for?"

"I don't remember," she said, "but not beets, I'm sure."

"Me, too," he said, laughing. "You would never ask for beets."

His laugh irritated her, and her irritation irritated her. To erase it, she tried to recall what she had ordered. On every dinner tray was a list of choices for the next day's meals but unless it was something special, she couldn't remember from one day to the next. Usually it was nothing special. "I just know I'd never ask for beets," she said again, shoving them to the side of her plate until one slid over the edge onto the tray.

"Oops," Dad said quickly, scooping the escaped beet back onto the plate and wiping the tray, as though it mattered. "There's other good stuff," he said, pointing it out as though she couldn't see for herself, looking down at the plate by looking up in the mirror.

The presence of beets had warped her appetite. The green lima beans and the lime Jell-O looked sickening with the red beets. "Do they think it's Christmas?" she asked. She'd chosen the kids' menu of hamburgers and pizza until she was sick of hamburgers and pizza and then started ordering from the regular menu. But perhaps she'd have to return to the kiddie food. She pushed the tray table as far away as she could reach. "Isn't there any black food?" she asked.

"Caviar," he said.

"Ooooh," she said, her stomach rolling at the thought.

"Not feeling any better?" he asked, her tall red-haired father with the concerned face and the smile.

Why had he reminded her? Beets had made her forget, but now the awful discomfort toward him was there again. She bet he and Mom both had talked with Dr. Gilder about her. What kinds of things did they say? she wondered. What did Dr. Gilder say?

"I wonder how much farther I can count?" she said, and she began again with 28,188, counting out loud.

"You're not going to eat?" he asked.

"Twenty-eight thousand eight hundred eighty-nine," she said as a chorus to his voice, his bass, hers soprano. "Twenty-eight thousand eight hundred ninety."

"I thought you wanted me to read," he said to her 28,191.

"Shall I play while you count?" he asked. As she didn't answer, except for counting, he leaned down and unzipped the cello case. So many times she had watched him settle the mahogany instrument between his knees, one hand on the slender neck and strings and one on the bow.

"Twenty-eight thousand eight hundred ninety-nine," she said, even while she thought mahogany, chestnut, russet, burnt sienna. As Dad bowed out the music, deep clear single notes and the mellow blending of double, triple notes, she composed numbers and colors into her own sonata. Janessa's Sonata in Sorrel No. 28,207. What was that he was playing, and why did it, too, irritate her? She always loved the way he disappeared into the flow of notes, as if sharing them from his insides out. She didn't want this sharing, she wanted to disappear, but she was stuck here on this bed as surely as if she'd been nailed. With a broken back and the Crutchfield tongs she *had* been nailed.

"I want you to read now," she said, to stop his music, his gliding arm. She grabbed at the numbers paper and wrote down her latest. Just 28,210. Not even to thirty thousand yet. It was such slow going.

Eyes closed, at one with the cello and the music, Dad continued playing. She chewed the inside of her lip and thought she would pop, like she wished that dumb balloon would pop.

"In a minute, Janessa," he said quietly, his voice as deep and mellow as the music floating from the cello.

Her concentration was shot, and her head refused to return to numbers. She examined the ceiling and her eyes ran into the pink-faced balloon, suspended in air a couple of feet below the ceiling now, nodding, nodding as if it understood her anguish. She kept her eyes on the balloon, feeling some small connection. Both she and this balloon were bound here in this room with no say-so about what happened to them. But Dr. Gilder said she had a choice, said she could make some of the rules. The idea did not fill her with any pleasure as it had, a little, when they were developing the raceway.

"Okay, sweetheart, now what do you want me to read?" Dad had finished the piece and, with long practiced motions, he nestled cello and bow back into the canvas nest and zippered them in.

Janessa chewed on her lips a moment, wanting to say nothing, do nothing. She no longer wanted him to read to her, just wished he'd go away.

"Mythology," she said, flopping her arm to the side of the bed, dangling it toward the book.

"Mythology. Wow. A hefty volume," he said, picking it up, lodging it on his knees.

"Did you or Mom tell me stories of Norse mythology when I was little?"

He scrunched up his face as if he were looking around inside his head for information. "Well, perhaps your mother did, but I don't think I ever did," he said. "I can't even think of any Norse mythology."

"Thor," she said, naming the only one she'd ever heard of before the other day.

"Oh, yes. Of course. The Thunder God." He nodded. "Who else?"

She told him about Tyr, Odin, Thor, Freya, and the days of the week, and about Asgard and the Rainbow Bridge, but not about Freyr and the *Skidbladnir*.

"Is that what you want me to read about?" He opened the book and started rustling pages.

"Yes," she said, "but especially about something called the Valkyries and a place called Valhalla."

"Is this for school?" he asked, and she heard the pleasure in his voice along with the soft flipping of pages.

"Well, yes, sort of," she said. Now his pleasure irritated her. What was wrong with her? She used to enjoy pleasing him. Now all she wanted to do was stamp her foot, which she couldn't do, and shout, "Go away and don't bother me!" which she wouldn't do. Not tonight, anyway. Not if she could help it.

"There's some stuff here about female spirits called Norns who spun the threads of destiny."

"No, Daddy, not Norns. Valkyries." She'd never heard of Norns. Whoever they were she didn't care. She had too much new stuff in her head already.

"Ah, here they are. 'The Valkyries were also dispensers of destiny. But their power extended only to one class of men, namely warriors.' "

Janessa clawed her fingers into the sheet, for she knew he was at the right spot, the scary part. He told her how the Valkyries went onto the field of battle and decided which side would win and which heroes would live or die.

"They decided?" she said, horrified at the image of Valkyries pointing fingers, saying, "You live" and "You die" and "You have your arm cut off."

"What is this teacher teaching you?" Dad asked. "I think that's enough of this." He closed the book.

"Nooo!" she said. "I have to know. I mean, I want to know."

"But Janessa," he began.

"I've been having dreams. Nightmares," she added quickly. "I thought maybe if I learned some things about them, it would stop the dreams."

"I'm having a talk with this teacher. Ms. Simpson. Is that her name?"

"No, Daddy," Janessa said. "I mean, yes, that's her name, but no, don't talk to her about it. She didn't start this."

"Then who did?"

"I did, I guess," she said. "I started it in my own head. That's why I was asking if you'd read Norse mythology to me when I was little. You, Mommy, Grandma, somebody must have. I need to know more about the Valkyries. And Valhalla. Please."

Sighing reluctantly he reopened the book. "Another Beethoven sonata would be better for you," he said.

She knew it wouldn't.

He'd found the page again. " 'They wore helmets, carried flaming spears, and rode flying horses whose manes dripped dew and hail. They could also turn themselves into swans and fly through the air and land on lakes and pools or in lonely forests,' " Dad read.

Ahhh, Janessa thought. Swans. The graceful, white image of swans was so different from the bloody march of the dead that a smidgen of her fear melted away.

Dad was shuffling pages, skipping around, reading here and there.

"Don't skip," Janessa said. "Read it to me."

"Sweetheart, there's not one section just about Valkyries and Valhalla, but various mentions of it here and there." He continued to read snatches, about the hall of the dead, where Odin held a celebration every night for the courageous who were killed in battle.

"Celebrating death?" Janessa shivered. "That's hard."

"Yes, it is," he said. "Most mythologies and religious beliefs celebrate death. You know that yourself, if you think about it. But I can tell you I would not have celebrated yours. I would have howled and kicked and screamed every

·110·

day for the rest of my life." And with the edge of the big book cupped in one hand he came to the bed and touched her hair, her cheek, and nuzzled her with kisses.

Comfort and discomfort swirled within her until it was all she could do to keep from howling herself, so she closed her eyes against it and against him and pretended to fall asleep. He stayed there by her, and she wondered if her eyelids fluttered, if he knew she was just bluffing.

While her eyes were still closed, Mom came in, and Janessa heard their whispered voices, but she didn't want to join them, so she kept herself removed with her hoax of sleep. Even when she heard her mother say, "I've got a sack full of silly sunglasses; do you know what she wants them for?" Janessa kept still. Her head gave her the number back and without letting her lips move, she moved numbers through her head, deciding to reach thirty thousand, so she could remember it without writing it down. She managed to get to 28,888 before, sick of eights, she stopped.

In the morning she didn't speak to anyone. No response to the good-morning chatter of the nurses as they checked her statistics for another day. No return remarks to the comments of the aide who rolled up yesterday's sheet, unrolled the fresh one, and tucked them both beneath her like feeding a piece of cardboard under a weathertight door and finally pulling it through from the other side. Nor did she let her eyes follow any of the movement in the room. At first, she'd stared at the balloon, sagging now, midway between ceiling and floor. As deflated and wrinkled as it was, it still wavered and moved and even bumped shoulders with the people bustling about the room, bringing breakfast trays, examining bones. So she just stared straight up. Easy enough. She pretended there was a royal-blue spot on the ceiling above her, like the life spot on a fiddler crab, and that if she didn't keep her eyes on it, the ceiling would fall in on her. Although she wouldn't mind if it did.

"You're a quiet one this morning," one would say. Or "Cat got your tongue?" No, she was tempted to say, the balloon has it, but she kept her silence. After a while, there was a little hubbub of alarm about her.

"Are you all right?" a nurse asked.

"Or are you just taking a day of silence?" asked another.

"Just give us one answer, that's all. We need to know."

"Are you all right? Just say yes if you are." The nurse lifted her arm and Janessa left it limp. They even examined her eyes, holding each open in turn with thumb and forefinger as if they weren't open already, then shining a penlight in. What did they see, she wondered? What could they tell about her? Or not tell?

Even when Dr. Gilder came she maintained her pose. There were ways, she was discovering, of separating herself from the world. He bounced in, saying, "Good morning, Janessa," and crossed the room and opened the blinds. As the sun hit her face, she felt her pupils contract, but she didn't even blink. Nor did she reach for his sunglasses, or remind him that he'd left them. Returning to the end of the bed, he seemed to know she wasn't speaking. He didn't mention sunglasses either, but looked silently at her chart. Had they written on it that she hadn't spoken to anyone today? Perhaps they had. He pulled up a chair and sat there near the foot of the bed without saying anything. If she looked, she knew she could see his head and shoulders. But she stared only at the blue spot.

"Black," she thought. The color of his clothes. The color of him. "Sable. Ebony. Inky. Sooty." Then she could think of no other names for black. With him accepting her silence and not chattering at her, it was harder to stay quiet than it had been with all the people trying to make her say something. That was odd. She would have thought it would be easier. She glanced up at her clock. It was going to be a long hour.

What was her last number? She would count. But she couldn't remember the last number and wouldn't reach for the paper on which she'd written it. Or had she written it? Didn't she go to sleep last night counting, trying to reach some easy-to-remember number? Her brain was in knots, but she didn't wrinkle her face. All she could remember were those interminable eights.

The thought of his sunglasses lingered and made her remember Mother's voice saying she'd brought a sack of sunglasses. She almost opened her mouth to ask Dr. Gilder to look for them, but she stopped herself. Mother had probably put them in the closet.

For the entire hour, she didn't see him or hear him, even when she listened for his breathing, even when she wondered if she'd dozed off and he'd tiptoed out. But finally he stood. Black, ebony, sable. Chocolate. How could she have forgotten chocolate? And licorice.

"You know I'm available to you if you want to reach me," he said, and he gripped her toes and gave them a small shake.

She jerked, gasped, and her eyes fogged, then focused.

"Oh, Janessa, I'm sorry," he said. "I'm so sorry!" He brushed the air above her toes, above her entire broken leg as if to erase what he'd done. "I meant this one," he said, gripping and shaking her other foot. "I meant this one. I'm so sorry. Are you okay?"

How could he have yanked on her broken leg like that? How could he have forgotten which leg? One was in traction, one was not, that was easy enough! Eyes on him now, she remained as still and quiet as when she had not been looking at him. This had been the most miserable hour she'd ever spent, she thought, and the quick, sharp pain of the unexpected joggling was a fitting end to it.

"Forgive me?" he asked.

When she didn't respond, he made an extravagant check to be sure he had her uninjured leg, patted her toes, and walked out without looking back.

After that, nothingness. She lay still, hands at her sides, eyes on the blue spot. Air current pushed the balloon until it hovered over the bed, over her chest as though in a staring contest with her. Finally, after all this time, it was in reach and she could bat it hard enough to pop it. But now she felt as sorry for it as she did for herself. Besides, her arms were like sodden timber and she couldn't lift them.

A nurse's aide, in her rose-colored dress, spouting red and pink words, brought lunch and set it on the rolling table and eased it across her. "Is this all right, honey? Can you see everything okay? Do you want me to help you?"

Janessa said nothing.

In a minute a nurse came in. "Go ahead with your lunch, Janessa. Your parents called to say that neither of them will be able to come help you with it today. Let me know if you need a hand." The nurse didn't even stay long enough for an answer.

Janessa flashed hot and cold, as though she'd had first scalding, then ice water pitched over her. They weren't coming? Neither of them? Her eyeballs burned but her blood was cold. She did not cry and she didn't move to touch her lunch. She was absolutely sure Dr. Gilder had called and told them not to come.

Rain lashed the window in silver streaks, which suited her mood. For a while she just stared at the storm, then pulled her work tray over and scrabbled for an origami paper. Dark blue. At first she simply looked at it and named colors. Midnight blue. Steel blue. Ultramarine. Indigo. Then, with deliberation, she began to fold until she had hull, mast, and sails. Holding the small ship in her hand, she sailed it back and forth across her body. Lingering in her mind was the thought of living in the orchard in Asgard and ignoring Valhalla. Sif would be her friend, she was sure of it.

Holding her breath, she began unfolding the blue boat. At the first trimming of the sails the *Skidbladnir* bulged into the room as though it had been waiting outside for her summons.

"Gladden, Janessa," Freyr said, looking at her from the deck.

"I want to go to Asgard," she said.

"You are afraid in Asgard," he said.

"I like the freedom of it," she said.

"Hmmm," he said. A pleased-sounding *hmmm*.

"Will they let me come? Will Odin let me come?"

"Come aboard," he said, lifting her. "We go inquire."

"You have new sunglasses," Freyr said as he set her aboard.

"Yes." These were Dr. Gilder's one-way glasses. She held her face up to Freyr and tapped the lenses. He stooped and peered.

"Ha," he said. "I see me. Like in water."

"I have sunglasses for everyone," she said, remembering. "I meant to bring them. Can I get them now?" She reached for the rail.

"In due time," he said. The sails were already full of wind, they were already on their way. "Loki is having grand fun with ones he has."

"You mean he's stolen them back from Sif?"

"Of course."

"Since he has those, maybe he'd leave these others alone."

"How little you know Loki," he said.

She shrugged. Maybe so, she thought, but if she had the chance, she would give the sunglasses anyway, even if Loki ended up with them all.

"Look," he said, looking out and down and stretching his arms to include everything. "World is beautiful in rain, aye?"

Rain, yes, it was raining. Out there. Down there. But not here on the *Skidbladnir*. When she looked down her eyes were bathed in glistening green, tops of trees and a green expanse of marsh with traceries of tidal creeks with no reflections in them. Marsh? Tidal creeks? She gulped and almost drew back, but stopped herself. Were they still over Hanover? Her eyes followed the ways they knew on land and there among the live oaks, pines, palms, and oleanders she picked out the courthouse, the school, the neighborhood, her street, her very house. Between her house and Lynn's was the live oak that grew like a bond, spreading its limbs over both houses. Lynn. Quickly, quickly, she looked for Lynn but there was no one moving on the streets, or in the yards, as though the place had been purged of people. School, she thought quickly, school! Her eyes flashed the blocks to school where she could not decipher Lynn among the antlike children scurrying about the school yard.

With another sweep of his arms Freyr said, "Farms and fields and even rocks are named after me throughout this land."

"In Hanover?" she said, astonished. She'd never heard of a Freyr anything in Hanover. In Hanover there were no rocks, except those imported for seawalls.

"Norway and Sweden," he said.

Even as she said "Huh?" she saw mountains rising from

the flatlands of Hanover. "I thought we were over Hanover."

"We were," he said, "but I am trying to find break in clouds."

"Oh," she said, surprised again. She knew the ship scooted through holes in the clouds, but she didn't know it was a necessity.

"Look," he said, and she had already looked when he added, "There is my burial mound."

She jerked back from the railing and crossed her arms. "But you're not dead," she said. "You're here."

"Been dead for centuries, I have," he said, laughing. "Past, present, future, all time is one. A fine burial mound, aye, Janessa? A door and three slots where people leave gifts to sustain me in afterlife."

She looked up and out at the unvaried gray sky, hoping they'd soon find a hole in the clouds. As though she'd willed it, the bland sky changed, whorled, spun a blue circle into the gray and the *Skidbladnir* swooped through.

Now she looked over the railing again. Instantly the Ice Mountains glittered in the distance. Some giant or other was striding across them, chasing or fleeing from something she couldn't see. Her heartbeat quickened. Asgard. The river. The Rainbow Bridge. The city of silver and gold.

As they approached the bridge, Heimdall, who saw to the end of the universe, was turned away pretending not to see them.

"Gladden, Heimdall," Freyr said to the back of Heimdall, as they drifted to shore and he began to lower the sails, fold down the masts. "Where's Odin?"

"Yggdrasil," Heimdall said.

Freyr nodded as though he understood the mumbled gibberish.

"What?" Janessa said, reaching out to rub Goldenbristle when the boar landed on deck as lightly as a leaf.

"The World Tree," Freyr said.

"Oh," she said, nodding, remembering that like everything else here the World Tree had a name. Even though she'd just heard it, she couldn't say it. It sounded like talking with your mouth full.

She had to run to keep up with the long strides of Freyr. When they were almost to the tree, she realized she could have ridden on the shoulders of Goldenbristle, who romped along beside them.

In the crest of the tree sat an eagle, flapping its wings and stirring things up. A quarrelsome-sounding squirrel ran up and down the length of the tree, from eagle to roots and back and forth again and again. In the lower branches and about the base of the tree were all manner of goats and deerlike creatures leaping about and nibbling tender shoots of the tree. And there with them was Sleipnir, Odin's eight-legged steed, browsing the tall, thick grasses.

Odin startled her as he stepped from the other side of the tree, because as big as he was, the tree was bigger. A herd of buffalo could be concealed behind this tree. Those crows flapped from his shoulders and the two wolves slavered at his knees.

"Gladden, Odin," Freyr said.

"Gladden. How was your autumnal tour?" Odin spoke to Freyr and didn't seem to notice Janessa.

"Aye, good, as every year," Freyr said.

"Did world accept your blessing?"

"Not entirely," Freyr said, "but I make anyway." He nodded now toward Janessa. Odin's one visible eye, brow raised, turned on her and his voice rumbled an enormous "Well?"

The question mark at the end was strong enough to blow her back to Hanover, but she raised her chest and shoulders and said, "I've come to ask if I can stay."

"Stay?" he said in a roaring voice like Thor. "You don't like us."

"I *do*," she said with emphasis. "I do. I love Freyr and the *Skidbladnir* and Goldenbristle and the Rainbow Bridge and Sleipnir and your gold rings and . . ."

"Except Freyr you are naming things," he said.

She was embarrassed. She should have said first of all that she liked him. But that would have sounded false and he would have known the falseness.

"But I do like you," she said. "It's a little scary because it's so different here. I'm not used to such, uh, large-sized things—trees, animals, people. And I don't know why you have such a horrible thing as the parade of the dead."

"You're right. You do not know," Odin said. "You do not know our kingdom. You're not brave enough for our kingdom."

Janessa sucked in her breath.

"Do you have wisdom beyond All-Father? You have both eyes." He brushed the hair away from his face, revealing the no-eye, the empty socket. "I trade eye for wisdom. What give you for yours?"

He looked as if he expected an answer, but Janessa was stunned speechless.

"While you are here, I grant protection," he said, opening a pouch and removing one of his rings. He slid it onto her finger where, as before, it shrank to fit. "But you may not stay. And when you go, you must find own way back to world of men."

She looked at Freyr in alarm. Freyr and Odin were looking at each other, nodding as if in agreement.

"All-Father not mean right this minute," Freyr said. "Come, walk me to Rainbow Bridge."

With her heart pounding in her throat, scarcely knowing he had hold of her hand, she trailed him to the Rainbow Bridge. As soon as they walked onto it, clouds of color curled about her legs and feet. As though it was on automatic her mind thought red, purple, blue, green, yellow, orange, red, purple, blue, green, yellow, orange. If any conversation took place between Freyr and Heimdall, she was unaware and just as unaware when Freyr left her there, on the bridge with Heimdall. She was still distracting herself with the color mists, naming intermediary colors, when Heimdall spoke.

"Someone approaches."

Janessa looked up, almost surprised to see herself here on the bridge, surprised to see Freyr gone, and certainly surprised to hear the quiet Heimdall speak. She looked all around, and saw no one approaching. If he could hear grass growing, she wondered how far away he could see someone approaching. Heimdall was peering out into the distance away from Asgard. Curious, she sat and clutched her knees, the colors—puce, plum, peacock—rising about her in iridescent fog. After staring into the distance for quite some time, she finally saw a dot. Then the dot became two dots, and eventually she could see they were one small dot and a smaller dot. Heimdall watched. Time passed swiftly even though the dots moved with incredible slowness. All-time and no-time. The dots acquired legs, arms, and heads, then became two people. Two men. No, a man and a boy. "A boy!" she said with delight. Everyone in Asgard seemed to be overgrown, even the few she'd seen, a couple of sons of Odin, who were spoken of as "children." Surprised at how happy she was to see someone her own size, she jumped up to go meet the boy, scattering rainbow dust as she went.

Heimdall halted them all with a booming word as the two approached the bridge. It wasn't "Who goes there," but that's what it meant.

"A giant is after my boy," the man said. "I have come for Odin's help."

Before Janessa could think "Good luck!" Heimdall had blown one muted note on his ram's horn, and Odin, wolves at his heels and ravens clinging to his shoulders, came galloping on Sleipnir.

"Oh, All-Father, can you help me?" the peasant cried,

spelling out a tale of losing a game of draughts with a giant and having to give his son for the winnings. Janessa opened her mouth in surprise and looked at the man and boy.

"The giant is coming," Heimdall said.

Janessa saw nothing, no one in sight across the plains, but she knew Heimdall must see him and hear footsteps heavier and more solid than those of the peasant and his son.

With a wave of Odin's hand, green shoots began springing from the earth, as in time-lapse photography. Odin scooped up the boy, who became a grain in Odin's hand. Stalks grew tall, formed heads of grain, then Odin set the single grain from his hand into one of the heads of grain.

"What is it? Wheat?" Janessa asked. The boy who had for so long looked like a dot, crossing the plain, had now truly turned into a dot before her eyes! And in the blink of an eye.

"Barley," said the peasant, nodding, and blinking his eyes.

Scooping up the peasant as he had the boy, Odin mounted Sleipnir. Eight legs leaping, they galloped away, horse, god, peasant, wolves, ravens, all.

The giant came on, now, faster than time. As though he knew what was in the fruited field, he drew his sword and, with wide slashing strokes, started threshing. When the stalks fell, he whacked them, splitting each barley head, scooping up grain and sifting it through his fingers.

Still on the down slope of the far side of the bridge, because she hadn't thought to move and now didn't dare,

Janessa shuddered at the sifting and flinched at each split. Heimdall put a hand on her shoulder and motioned her to come up higher on the bridge.

After a while, roaring at not having found what he was looking for, the giant stomped away.

As soon as the giant was out of sight, here came Odin, Sleipnir, and all, Odin leaning out and down from the eight-legged mount, like any trick rider. Out of an entire field of rubble, he plucked up one grain. By the time he was upright on the horse's back, it was the boy he had, holding him by the back of his leather tunic as Sleipnir frolicked away.

Taking them home, Janessa thought, wishing she could go, wishing he'd grabbed her up as well, to take her home. Or to take her home with the boy. She would like the ride, like playing with the boy, like being a part of the magic. Glancing at Heimdall, she was surprised to see him looking off in various directions, on guard duty and apparently unimpressed with what had just happened. She guessed these sorts of things happened often enough in Asgard to be ordinary.

What fun, but scary, too, being on her own on the back
of the golden boar. Dr. Gilder's sunglasses on her face, she
gripped Goldenbristle's ear with one hand while the other
dangled and stroked the smooth gold shoulder. Over the
Rainbow Bridge, as she raised that hand to wave to Heimdall, the ring of Odin flashed in the sun. Protection. Was
it? Heimdall didn't return her wave. Should she stay right
here and stick like glue to Freyr, whether he liked it or
not?

When she'd asked Freyr to take her to visit the boy, he'd

told her she'd have to go by herself. He couldn't, he said, spend every minute with her. But time meant nothing here. The peasant and the boy had taken forever and no time to emerge from dots. Freyr himself had told her that all times were one, so what difference did it make to him? His refusal scared her at first, and hurt her feelings. Was he against her, too? Would they really make her find her own way home? And how could she do that? But if she had to make her own way, what difference did it make, then, if she stayed with Freyr or not? She was abandoned, in any case. It would be fun to see this person, here, who was her size. Besides, she did have the protection of Odin. He promised. She rubbed the ring against her chin. Now, here she was, in the middle of the magic, soaring above all on the back of a golden boar. And there was no parade of the dead. Instead, below her were rivers of flowers.

Then there were grainfields and thatched huts. Midgard, the world of men. Not her world of men but some ancient world, out of history books. Amazing, this thing about all time being one. If her parents could see her now, out of the binding tongs of the hospital bed, would they be happy for her? Would they want her to stay here where she could be well and free? Would they want to be here with her? If there was so much magic here, perhaps, no matter what Odin said, she could find a way to stay here and to bring them here, all of them—Mom, Dad, Donna and Billy, and Lynn, too.

In all-time, she recognized the estate of the peasant that Freyr had described to her. Look for a river where it broadens to the sea, he had said, and columns of crops growing at the rim of the river. And there was the river, and the sea, shimmering like aquamarine crystal. And there were the fields, with Goldenbristle's shining rippling across the combed rows. And there was the man himself, not looking up in wonder at the girl on the golden boar. There was an expansive stone house, a stone silo, and a series of stone fences, but no sight of the boy. When Goldenbristle touched ground, and she slid off and walked toward the man, he saw her immediately.

"Just who I needed," he said, as though not at all surprised to see her. "You're the girl from the end of the Rainbow Bridge, aren't you? Where's Odin? I need Odin. The giant is still after my boy."

"Where is he?" she asked, meaning both the giant and the boy. For all her new spirit of adventure, she wasn't ready for giants. If only she were still at the end of the Rainbow Bridge in sight of Heimdall and in range of any of the others who weren't off to wherever it was they went off to. Even if they didn't want her there, she would feel safer.

The ground trembled and the peasant cried out, "Here he comes! Oh, Hoenir, help me!"

Janessa looked for escape, but didn't see Goldenbristle, nor did the boar come. Though the giant was not in sight, the ground shook with his approaching steps.

What appeared instead of Goldenbristle or the giant was a Loki-sized, Odin-sized, Freyr-sized person, neither giant nor regular man.

"Are you from Asgard?" she asked, assuming he must be one of the gods she hadn't met.

"Aye, gladden. And you?" the new one said to Janessa.

"From the world of men," she said. Their words were muffled by the loud, urgent pleas of the peasant. "But I'm under the protection of Odin," she shouted.

"Aye, that I see," said this Hoenir, regarding the ring. "I heard about Odin turning you to barley."

"No, that wasn't me," Janessa said, sorry for the boy but not sorry for the man who was in such fear for his son. How could he have wagered his son in a game of draughts? It reminded her of the story of Jephthah from the Bible, and she'd never liked Jephthah much after that, no matter how many explanations she was given.

The giant came into view across the river, and plunged, wading, into the water. Hoenir swooped Janessa to his shoulder and rushed in long strides to where the river spilled into the sea. Several swans glided along near the shore. As the water-thrashing giant splashed downriver toward them, two of the swans waddled out of the surf toward Janessa. In spite of herself, she almost laughed because she saw there were seven swans. Seven swans a-swimming, right out of a song! She was mesmerized by this combination of fear and tranquillity. On the day she was snatched from the store and thrown from the car the sky was a brilliant and cloudless nothing-bad-can-happen blue.

"Become a feather!" said the new god, Hoenir, snapping his fingers.

Quickly she looked to see who he was snapping at, and there was no one but her and Hoenir and the approaching giant. Before she could say "How do you think I can do that?" she was a feather, looking down from the head of a swan.

The giant reached out one huge hand and grabbed just that swan and flung it about and wrung its neck. As he roared and searched every feather, one small, downy Janessa-feather drifted, unseen, to the water. Bobbing along in the current, she could still see and hear, but she was white and fluffy and floating down a river! When she'd thought she wanted to be in the middle of the magic, she hadn't meant to be this much in the middle of it! What if the magic didn't reverse, as it had when the boy was turned back from a grain of barley? How had she gotten into this just from wanting to see someone her size? Did they—Hoenir and the giant—think she was the boy? And the father! How awful he was to use her as a decoy.

As the giant roared and tore the poor swan apart feather by feather, Hoenir scooped the tiny plume from the flowing river and held it loosely in his hand.

"You had your winnings," the giant bellowed to the peasant, who was standing some distance back. "I will have mine. I have powers. I be watching you." He splashed angrily downriver to sea as though the ocean were a shallow pond.

"Here is boy back," Hoenir said, when the giant was out of sight, and he set the feather on the sand. Just as the falcon had gained legs and became Loki, the feather sprouted legs and became Janessa, complete with sunglasses.

"But I'm not his boy!" she said in protest, but the god was gone without even a "Grace be with you," and she was there with only the peasant.

"Thank you," he said, looking relieved.

All she could think of to say was her very huffiest "Huh!"

No longer in the least interested in playing with the boy, she called for Goldenbristle, who didn't come. Freyr whistled for the boar, but Janessa's mouth was too dry to purse up a whistle. Grinding her heel into the sandy soil, she turned her back on the peasant and started down the shoreline, following swans.

"Please stay," the peasant said, in the gentlest of voices.

"Huh!" she said again, as loudly as she could. The witch from Hansel and Gretel had somehow gotten into this story in the form of a peasant and she wasn't staying around to find out if she ended up in an oven. As she stalked along the beach, more angry than afraid, she almost forgot where she was. This was so like the beach at home, on Golden Isle, near Hanover. Home. Suddenly, she remembered where she was and wondered how she'd get back—home. Or even to Asgard, which she had, perhaps stupidly, left.

"Freyr, help me," she said. Wasn't that how the peasant had summoned Hoenir, just by asking? But no Freyr appeared. Nor any golden boar. And there was no paperlike material here from which to fold a small boat to make the magic happen. "Hoenir, help me." Her feet followed the frothy rim of foam the waves left on the sand and the swans glided along just beyond the breakers, leading on. A smile popped to her face. Had she crossed a time band? Was she home? Were the swans leading her home? Freyr had said she'd find a way. This water was dark, not aquamarine like a few minutes or all-time ago. And the waves were low and gently fluted, not huge crashing rollers. Like home. Like Golden Isle. Was she home, in her own Midgard, but still moving, walking, not tonged and weighted to a hospital bed? Holding out her arms she turned circles and scalloped the sand at the leading edge of the waves. This was the best magic of all.

Then, incredibly, there was the peasant ahead of her. How had he crossed into her time band? She did not want him here. How had he gotten ahead of her by following her? Arms still out, she reversed her direction and whirled away from him.

"Wait," he said. "I need one of the gods. The giant is still after my boy."

One of the gods? Had she not, after all, crossed over? "Call them, then," she said, scuffing her foot in the sand. "You were the one who summoned them before." Why did he think she would help? Didn't he know she probably *couldn't* help, even if she would?

"Oh, Loki, help me!" the peasant cried. The giant was sloshing in from the sea.

Abruptly, Janessa realized she was still the likely alternate. "Yes, Loki, help!" she cried, looking for a place to hide, but among marsh grass and sea oats there were no choices.

At once Loki was there, changing her into something without even commanding first. What was she, a tadpole egg? One small dot among hundreds. Why did they keep turning things into dots? Suddenly she was in a moist, dark place being sloshed about. Everything smelled fishy. Was she a fish egg? Caviar? Was she inside the belly of a fish? There was a jolt, and a slit of light which widened, then the thick fingers of the giant reached in and scooped up the eggs. One by one he sorted through them, counting as he went. Janessa hoped there were a million eggs, because she knew how hard it was to count to a million.

The mass of eggs quivered as the giant searched through them. Though just as immobile as if Crutchfield-tonged to the bed, Janessa-as-egg thought "Wiggle, wiggle, wiggle" as the giant jiggled the eggs in his hand. Instantly, she whoopsed between his third and fourth fingers, slid loose from the glutinous whole, and landed with a plop in the sand. As soon as she hit, her legs and feet appeared under her. Returned to her normal shape, she was standing in the shadow of the giant. For one quick moment, she thought maybe the safest place might be right here, so close to him he couldn't see her. Then she ran.

The sun was fierce and she was grateful for the still-present sunglasses as she ran like wind, like waves, like wildfire. The ground shook at his pounding steps behind her as she bolted across the firm wet sand near the water rather than on the loose dry sand near the dunes. From her racing days she knew not to waste one millisecond on looking back. From the weight and speed of the giant's steps the earth boomed like thunder. The force of it knocked her down but, scrambling like a crab, she kept moving. In that position, she managed to glimpse beneath her arm, certain that his hand would be at her ankle, but she saw he had fallen, too. He was sprawled on the sand, his head and scrabbling arms so near that the shock of it bounced her up and she kept running.

"You can stop running now," a voice said, and in spite of herself, she took the chance of looking.

The giant was not on the sand but in it, up to his neck and clawing to climb out. The more he clutched at sand the deeper he sank until his head disappeared. Sand, following the laws of sand, flowed into the pit and covered him.

Standing at the edge of the dunes, up to his knees in sea oats, with the chartreuse sunglasses perched on his nose, laughing, laughing, laughing, was Loki.

Some time passed before Janessa saw the humor.

G ladden, Janessa. Big eyes saved you," Loki said.

"My sunglasses?" she asked, reaching up and touching the frames, and laughing, because he looked so absolutely ridiculous with those glamour glasses perched on his nose.

"Aye. Sun blinded giant, make run slow. Give time to make trap, make him not see trap. With big eyes, you see and keep feet on firm wet sand, so run fast."

"Maybe," she said, thinking he just didn't know how fast she could run. "I was going to bring you your own pair of big eyes," she said.

"You were?" he said, surprised and pleased.

"You liked them so much I thought if you had your own maybe you'd let me have mine back."

"Aye," he said, "I might."

"I was going to bring some to everyone," she said, thinking, as she said it, that it was pointless to say it. There would be no more going and coming, no bringing of sunglasses. And she had to find her own way home.

She looked around and wondered how to begin. Since she entered this time band at Asgard, perhaps she should leave from Asgard. Would they let her do that? "Will you take me back to Asgard?" she asked.

"I have appointment with Elves of Ivaldi," he said. "Have got mitself into situation."

She nodded and rolled her eyes. "Yes, I've heard about some of your situations." She was thinking of Sif's hair and all the fine gifts the elves had made for him to give so he could redeem himself with his fellow gods. Without one of those gifts, the *Skidbladnir,* she wouldn't even be here. But here she was, and now she was in her own "situation."

"Got mitself in it this time," he said.

They were standing on the sand, waves whirring steadily. She might be standing on Golden Isle, talking with Lynn.

"Elves will revoke gifts if I do not bring what they want. Gifts of gold already revoked."

She looked at her hand, and the ring of Odin still glinted in the sun.

"Has lost power," Loki said.

"Lokiiii!" Janessa said, in a howl. A sense of danger

floated around her in the rays of the sun. Goldenbristle! One of the gifts of gold. No wonder he didn't come! She longed for the safety of Asgard, or even the hospital room and the security of Crutchfield tongs. She would need some of Asgard's magic to get home, she was sure of it, even if she had to figure it out for herself. What if the elves revoked it all?

In horror, she asked, "What have you done?" As though the world still went on, the waves crashed a hundred feet out, rolled in, and flattened out on the sand until even the dark water paled and became transparent. Janessa stared at the water as though she might see something important, but when Loki didn't answer, she became even more frightened. Loki had magic, too, so it was hard to imagine what he had done and what the elves might want that he could not provide.

Almost in a whisper, she asked, "What do they want?"

"Breath of cat, noise of fish," he said.

"Oh, Lokiii," she said. Hopelessness shuddered through her. For one split second, she had thought she would help Loki get whatever it was the elves wanted, but where would even Loki get such things? She had been turned into a feather and into a fish egg, but both of those were actual things that could be seen and touched, and found. While in the belly of the fish, she didn't recall hearing any sounds of the fish.

"Or live blood sacrifice," he said.

With a jolt, she saw visions of the Valkyries bringing the bloody dead to Valhalla, felt that bloody arm falling against her. Suddenly, it was her arm. If she didn't get back to Asgard, she would wind up in the middle of Loki's mischief, she knew it. She would be the blood sacrifice.

"Can't you take me home first?" she asked. "Back to Asgard, I mean?" She touched Odin's ring, rubbing the birds and wolves engraved there, willing their protection. Being in Asgard was her only protection.

"Come on, I will take," he said in a talking-to-a-baby voice.

She cringed. She'd had enough of that in the hospital. Instead of complaining or saying thank you, thank you, thank you a dozen times, she managed to say, "You will? Thanks." It was good not to show him her fear, even though she had it. And what did the time matter to him, anyway? He'd have her back in Asgard and be at his appointment with the Elves of Ivaldi without a minute passing.

Loki hunched his shoulders, jutted his head forward, raised his arms, elbows first, like a bird raising its wings, and he became a bird, heavy-headed, with an enormous beak.

"A pelican!" Janessa said, amazed.

"Pelican is fun," Loki said.

"Ohh," she said, "you can talk while you're a bird!"

"Aye," he said.

She wondered if she could have talked while she was a feather or a fish egg. It had seemed like a time to be silent, so it hadn't even occurred to her. As the pelican leaned down and she climbed onto its shoulders, the thought of a talking fish egg almost made her giggle.

How many times had she watched the pelicans flying over Golden Isle, sometimes high, sometimes skimming the surf, flying in single file if there was more than one. And here she was, so close to the waves that she could see down into the dark water more than she would have thought possible.

Her hair ruffled in the wind and suddenly she thought of Sif. The Elves had revoked the gifts of gold. Sif's hair! Was Sif bald? Janessa felt a double pain—one for Sif for having now lost her hair twice and the other against herself because she hadn't thought of Sif first, but only of herself.

Without warning Loki dove for a fish, crashing into the water, almost tossing Janessa off by the force of the splash. She clung so tightly to the neck feathers, she thought she might pull them loose and still land in the sea. They landed safely, though this was one pelican, she thought, which deserved to be plucked bald. Loki-pelican bobbed on the waves, tilted his beak upward as though for his next trick he might catch a cloud. As the bird swallowed, Janessa felt the bulge of the caught fish sliding down its throat.

"Warn me, next time," she said. But the bird didn't answer. Fish swallowed, he spread those powerful wings and lifted them, dripping, springing from the sea. Janessa was sodden and shivering in the breeze. Evidently he never considered the fact that she didn't have the warmth of feathers. But why should that surprise her? Apparently he didn't consider anything much except his own cleverness and pleasure.

Still, as when she was on the *Skidbladnir,* or that brief time aboard Goldenbristle, she was enchanted with the overall view from above. Out and up was endless sky and off in the distance was the Rainbow Bridge and the World Tree, looming large even from this far away. As she turned her head this way and that, looking down at oceans, at rivers, at hills and valleys, she saw the Ice Mountains, home of the Frost Giants. Fear leaped inside her. For assurance, she looked toward Asgard, the Rainbow Bridge, the World Tree, and was startled to see they were no closer.

"Where are you taking me?" she asked. She knew the answer the instant she asked the question, before his silence confirmed it. The only sound was that of the whooshing air, stirred by strong wings, and her own whooshing blood. Blood that would soon be involved in a sacrifice. What had Loki said they wanted? Noise of a fish? Would they accept the noise of her rushing blood without having to take her actual blood?

At last they set down in a stony forest. The webbed feet and squat pelican legs returned to long Loki legs as he touched ground and Janessa slid herself off the pelican's back. She wanted to run as she had when, as a fish egg, she'd plopped to the sand of the beach, but she knew there was no fleeing Loki.

"Business with Elves of Ivaldi," he said, answering the question she asked so many skies ago.

"You said you'd take me to Asgard," she said angrily,

wondering where she was in the world, and in what world. The sky, so endless just moments ago, was now piebald, shafts of brilliant light piercing through tree leaves.

"I said only, 'I will take.' "

She didn't recall, but if that's what he'd really said, she saw how clever and mean he was. How had she been so charmed by him? Even, yes, on this most recent journey on his pelican back.

"Come meet elves," he said, and even as she drew back in refusal, he moved a boulder and shoved her ahead of him into a small, dark cave.

Even with daylight flooding from above, Janessa could just barely see the top step of this stairway into the realm of the Elves of Ivaldi. Her initial fright turned to horror when she realized Loki had rolled the boulder back into place with her inside and himself outside, and then she couldn't even see the top step.

"Loki! Loki!" she cried, shoving uselessly against the rock. For a moment, the only answer was silence and darkness. Then a shrill, chilling voice from far below demanded,

"What vermin is invading Ivaldi?"

Janessa leaned back against the stone, almost expecting

it to give way behind her and let her out. When it did not, she rubbed Odin's ring and thought, "Odin, Freyr, Thor, Heimdall, Hoenir, Freya, Sif, help me." Anyone but Loki, who obviously was not helping. Peering into blackness and seeing nothing, she remembered her sunglasses, removed them but still saw only darkness.

"Avow yourself," the voice charged from not so far below.

This creature would be upon her before she knew it. She wished for cat eyes and courage as she reached out to touch the dark. The cavern walls were slick with moisture. Exploring with one foot, she felt a drop below her.

"I—I—I'm not invading," she managed to say, her voice echoing "vaa-ding, vaa-ding, vaa-ding" into the hollow. She slid the sunglasses inside her tunic, with one earpiece dangling outside like a clip.

"Advance," the voice ordered and Janessa retreated, trying to meld herself through stone the way the *Skidbladnir* entered and exited the hospital room. But she was flesh, and it was stone, and nothing melded.

"Advance!" the voice commanded, and she sat down in weakness but stretched her foot out and down and there was a ledge. With one hand on the cavern wall, she slid herself down one level.

Now a chorus of voices cried, "Advance!"

Janessa grimaced and closed her eyes as though to shut out what she could not see. Clenching herself against being seized, she tapped her feet out and below to the edge of each succeeding step. With her hand against the cavern wall she bumped herself down, down, and down until she was sitting on the bottom of the cave.

"Avow yourself," the chorus said, and she felt their breath in her face.

Now there was nowhere to go but up, so she stood up to keep from being hovered over. She still couldn't see them but she could feel them there, pressing against the darkness.

"It is I, Janessa," she said, her voice as squeaky as a mouse.

"Vanessa, what venture have you in the caverns of Ivaldi?" This voice caromed off the cavern walls, saying, "valdi, valdi, valdi," and she could feel the breath of it on her face.

"I've, uh, Loki sent me," she said, deciding to claim Loki as an ally rather than say he shoved her into the cave. He had been in alliance with them before, even if he was in trouble with them now.

"Is Loki above?"

Certain that the pelican had flown, she said, "No, Loki is not above."

"Did you bring the voice of a fish?"

"The what?" she said, and instantly there was a murmur of the invisible voices. All these voices and not one of a fish. She'd been so frightened of the blood sacrifice, she'd forgotten there were other things they wanted. What from a cat? Its purr? Could she make them think she had it? Knowing she couldn't, she put one foot behind her, on the stair, but someone gripped her elbow and pulled her down again.

"Move along, move along," said the attendant voice as though she might not move, with him nearly dragging her along. She managed to keep her feet going fast enough to keep her balance, and as her eyes grew accustomed to the dark, she saw they were in a tunnel. Or no, it wasn't her eyes adjusting but that the walls of the cave glowed dimly, though she saw no lights or torches. A small figure, some-one not quite as tall as herself, but heavier and immensely stronger, was pulling her along and some others were be-hind, and the iron-gripping one kept saying, "Move along, move along," as if somehow she otherwise wouldn't.

"Loki brought this Vanessa," he said as they entered an open chamber where hot coals glowed from a fire.

"He's diminutive, like us," one said, and they clustered around, faces pale as paper, circling her, examining her.

"We have heard there were boys, but we have never seen one before."

She started to say "I'm a girl," but she was speechless. Since being mistaken for the peasant's son had so nearly gotten her devoured by a giant, she wanted to make the point. But in this case, she supposed it would make no difference.

"Verily, you are a nice size," said one elf with admira-tion.

"We live in a world of giants," said another.

"A valuable sacrifice," said another, and they all sighed in pleasurable agreement.

"A fine enough voucher for Loki's debt," said someone else, to collective sighs of agreement.

She noticed there were, astonishingly, seven elves. She counted again to be certain. After the seven swans, this was too much irony and she saw no humor. These were not the benevolent dwarves of a fairy tale. One of them had said the word—sacrifice. Though she would like to regain the gifts of gold, and would certainly like to retain the remaining gifts—especially the *Skidbladnir,* for Freyr— a boat and a boar were not worth her life.

"I—I—no," she said, trying to gain her voice, trying to think, trying not to show her fear. "I am not valuable." And her own words mixed with theirs reminded her that a worthy sacrifice must have value. "I'm not valuable," she said again. If these elves were anything like the gods of Asgard, they treasured courage. "I'm not valuable," she repeated. "I am very afraid."

One of the elves spat and they all stepped back, staring at her in revulsion.

"No valor?"

"Did Loki verify this sacrifice?"

"Did you not know it is the most vaulted favor to be sacrificed?"

"An honor only for the brave."

"Where is the knave Loki? Trying to deceive us again!"

The elves spoke angrily among themselves, and finally Janessa found her own voice.

"I am not the sacrifice," she said.

At this, they stopped their chatter and all seven looked at her in irate puzzlement.

She repeated her statement and they continued their stares.

"Why have you veered from our language? We no longer divine your words."

"What?" she said, and now she stared in bewilderment. What did they mean, why had she veered from their language? She was speaking the same as before, her language, the only language she knew.

"Why are you voicing words we cannot understand?" There was more passionate murmuring among them.

Would their next move be to thrust her into the fire, worthy or unworthy? Could she do anything to distract them? To gain time? Wasn't that what you were supposed to do? Gain time? When she was with the man in the car there was pure blind terror from beginning to end, with never a chance to think. This might end up even worse, but she was attempting to think.

"What vile thing is Loki up to?" one elf asked her.

"I don't know what Loki is up to," she said, trying to sound halfway calm. Would half-brave be enough to help her, but not enough to qualify as a valuable sacrifice?

"Why do you vex us? Voice our language! Speak Ivaldi!" they demanded.

"I don't know your language!" she shouted, frightened into anger herself.

Again they lapsed into a hubbub, then surrounded her, plucking at her as though they would pick her to pieces, like Odin's crows. One of them grabbed her hand and Odin's ring flashed in the firelight.

All stopped. The silence and stillness exceeded all-time. "Odin vouches for you?" one said, finally.

Her breath was locked so tight within her that it was a moment before she could release it. She nodded her head and said quietly, "Odin vouches for me."

There was a collective sigh of relief, theirs first, then hers. In a rush of understanding she knew that they, too, had been afraid. They had not known what lurked on the stairway at the entrance of their cavern. They had not known her powers. Surely, now, they knew she had no power, since her only power had been in the protection of this ring, and they'd revoked it. Apparently, they either feared or trusted Odin. But why did they trust Loki? They made their own magic, they didn't need Loki.

"Why did you stop voicing our Ivaldi language?" one asked.

"I never voiced your Ivaldi language," she said, using their phrasing, trying to maintain their fragile balance. "I only voiced my own language. I don't know your Ivaldi language."

"But you spoke Ivaldi," they insisted. "Then you halted speaking Ivaldi and we could not perceive your words."

It was her turn to stare as she tried to see through them, tried to see what she didn't understand and what they hadn't understood. The furor had arisen when she declared she wasn't a valuable sacrifice. Did they simply refuse to hear words that went against their wishes?

"I will try to speak Ivaldi," she said, terror still at her

throat in spite of the mood of relief. The elves had relaxed and were sitting down here and there in the chamber, as though for a social visit. She, however, was not invited to sit.

"Did you bring the vitality of a cat, then?"

So they still wanted something. Of course. They knew she had not brought the noise of a fish and that she would not make a pure-enough sacrifice. How could she stall them and keep them settled? She had to say something that pleased them or they wouldn't hear.

"I don't have the vitality of a cat," she said, "But I have wondered about why you involve yourselves with Loki if he's such a villain." Since they were upset with Loki, she thought perhaps she could align herself with them against him. The brief twinge she'd had about her selfishness, while on the back of the pelican, was gone. This was not about restoring Sif's golden hair, but about restoring herself to daylight, to Asgard, to the safety of the hospital room and even the security of the Crutchfield tongs.

The Elves were nodding, smiling. "Ah, the villain. But a most felicitous villain, would you not avow?"

The hovering hummingbird came to mind. She remembered her delight in his magic, and his playfulness, but did that make up for treachery? She could not answer, because she would say she did not avow, and her disagreement would set them off again.

"Valor doesn't stand alone without wit and vivacity," one of them said.

"Sunlight which is vital to you can be fatal to us. We

are elves of darkness. We have poor vision in the light. So, through Loki, we have a vent to the upstairs world. He brings us vistas . . ."

"Perspectives."

"Discoveries."

"Revelations."

"Levity."

"Yes, levity. Frivolity. A most valuable thing." The laughter of the elves glittered through the chamber as bright as firelight.

"And for our magic, Loki provides us with things we can't find for ourselves in that too-bright upstairs world. Veiled and vaporous things, things that are found in the void where things aren't found."

Stunned by their words and her own sudden light, and having scarcely more breath than a cat herself, she said, "I have something more valuable than the breath of a cat."

Clutching the earpiece of the sunglasses, she drew them from the neckline of her tunic, and held them out as an offering.

"Visors," she said, for she had also caught on to their language. It was the V's they required. "They'll increase your vision in the light."

Quicker than Loki, they snatched the sunglasses from her and took turns putting them on and peering around.

"Visors?"

"Visors?"

"Visors?" they said in turn.

"The fire starts to vanish," one said.

"Yes, and some of the sunlight vanishes, too," Janessa said. "You could find the veiled and vaporous things yourselves, without Loki."

One of the elves gave an openmouthed laugh of delight.

"We could find the veiled and vaporous Loki!"

The elves jumped and hopped and clapped and shrieked with pleasure.

In a relishing, washing-hands motion another elf said, "We have want of Loki."

"Everyone wants Loki," Janessa said, remembering Thor's rage.

"The silver-tongued mischief-maker takes advantage wherever he can," said another.

"Whatever happens to him will be too good," said yet another, and in spite of what Loki had gotten her into, Janessa felt a qualm about what she'd now gotten him into.

Still hopping and clapping, the elves all herded toward the door. "We will surprise Loki in his reverie," they said in chorus.

"Perhaps you should try the visors first," Janessa said, not wanting them to harm themselves, and also wishing she could think of something to save Loki's skin.

"Yes, I will take leave," said the one who had the glasses, and as he disappeared the others waited, still gathered by the door.

Lip between her teeth, she wondered why she was even worried about Loki's skin. He never seemed to worry about anyone else's, and he seemed to take care of his own quite well. But she reminded herself that there was more here than just Loki and Janessa. There was Goldenbristle and Odin's ring and all the other treasures of the gods. If Thor lost his hammer, that wouldn't be good for Loki's skin!

Thor would tear Loki to pieces as brutally as the giant had shredded the swan. She shivered at the thought of having been so near that slaughter.

Here came the elf back with a tooth-showing grin. "Visor works," he said. "But there is only one visor." He waggled the sunglasses at his mates.

"Vaahhhhh." They all groaned in surprise and sadness, and quarreling broke out about which one should go, each claiming to be the strongest or the swiftest or the most far-seeing.

"We shall resolve with coals," one said, and bare-handed they each drew a hot coal from the fire and set it on the hearth and stood watching as the coals glowed like dragon's eyes. One by one, the smoldering coals grew dim until only one showed fire. The elf who'd plucked that coal picked it up, tossed it, caught it, and slammed it back into the fire with such force sparks sprang up, like the orange mist from the Rainbow Bridge. At once the sunglasses were handed to him.

"Go with vigor of all," the other elves said together. Huddling, they clasped hands and arms as though exchanging strength.

Out of the room he went and Janessa followed. This was her time to leave, to go back to the light which was life to her.

"You, Vanessa, halt," she was told in a commanding voice.

"But, I—?" She gestured after the departing elf.

"You, Vanessa, sit. Wait."

She sat, staring at the doorway, listening to the rush of her blood and the clangor of the footsteps until they diminished in the distance. She concentrated on watching for a shaft of light when he moved the stone at the entrance, but minutes passed and the only light was the glimmer of the fire, as it licked at the shadows in the cave. They were so deep within the stony cavern of the earth and the elves were so quiet with waiting that there was no sound at all, not their breathing or her own. Even the fire had gone mute. Her head fell to her chest. She was going to be trapped here with them, after all, in failure if they didn't find Loki, with them and Loki if they did find him. There would be too much cleverness for her poor wits.

She was so deep within the stony caverns of herself that she almost didn't hear anything when there was something to hear. The clamoring, peppery Loki, arms bound to his body with a cocoonlike thread, was being shoved into the chamber by the elf. The elf was now proudly wearing two pairs of sunglasses, including the chartreuse ones which he immediately removed and passed around.

"Janessa!" Loki said. "You did this to me."

He couldn't have said anything worse to make her lose the sympathy she had been building for him.

"Loki!" she snapped back. "You did this to me!"

"No evasive communication," an elf commanded, sounding grim even while he took his turn with the newest pair of sunglasses. "Voice only in our language."

Janessa looked at Loki, feeling the same "Huh!" she'd felt earlier toward the peasant. "I will voice your language," she said, feeling it safer to cooperate. Had Loki alerted the gods in Asgard to her peril?

"How did you learn their language?" Loki asked.

"Do you crave to be one-eyed, like Odin?" an elf said, picking a coal from the fire and threatening Loki.

"Do I thereby derive wisdom?" Loki said, vanishing right before their eyes. The threads which had bound him held his shape for a moment, then fell in a fragile heap. "Try catching a fly to deprive it of its vision." His voice came from the midst of loud, aerial buzzing as he zoomed about the chamber.

"One small fly will not evade us," said one of the elves, gesturing toward the doorway, which was covered with a network of silver threads, like a spider's web. This elf now had on the chartreuse sunglasses, Janessa noted. It was as though they were developing a new communications system and only he who had on the chartreuse sunglasses could speak. "Perhaps you will buzz around in the caves of Ivaldi forever."

The fly landed on Janessa's nose and when she involuntarily brushed it away, it landed in her hair by her ear.

"I'll get us out of this," the fly buzzed in her ear.

As well he should, Janessa thought, since he'd gotten them into it. As suddenly as she'd had the first idea about the sunglasses, she now had another.

"I can get you more visors," she said. Instantly, she had their attention.

"More visors?"

"I can get you as many visors as you want," she said,

hoping they wouldn't want a million. Or, in fact, more than six. She'd just had a flash vision of the bagful of sunglasses she'd forgotten. She had asked Mother for six pairs. "I'll have to voyage to my world to get them."

"How do we receive these visors? You may not return to Ivaldi."

"I vow to return," she said.

Vigorously, they shook their heads. "You cannot invade Ivaldi again, Vanessa. Loki has aggrieved us by bringing you here."

"I am aggrieved, too," she said sharply, just barely remembering to use their language instead of puffing out another "Huh!" If anyone was invaded, she thought, it was she!

"How do you voyage to your world?"

"I voyage with Freyr on one of your valuable gifts, the *Skidbladnir*," she said. "Freyr can convey the visors." She was dismayed at more vigorous shaking of heads.

"We receive only Loki. No others voice our language. And you, Vanessa, but you may not return because we cannot have someone else our size in the vicinity."

What? Janessa thought. Did they think she had their powers because she was no taller than they were? And the language, yes, she remembered Odin saying that only Loki could communicate with the Elves of Ivaldi. Loki had kept the simple secret of their language to himself. And where was that fly now? She looked around but it was impossible to spot a silent fly in the dimness of the cave.

"I can voyage to my world with Loki," she said. "He will convey the visors to you." Surely, surely, that would satisfy them. And she supposed Loki had the powers to get her there.

All elf heads looked around and all eyes stopped on the fly. Being accustomed to the dark, they had no trouble finding him.

"I've never been to that other world," said the fly. "Would be in vain if I lost way."

The elves giggled.

"You have never lost your way."

"Even so, a magic coal will guide you," one said, and he snatched a coal from the fire and tossed it among the other elves while he spun a gold net with a silver handle to carry it.

"As for you, Vanessa, you will send the visors by Loki and never return to our world, neither Ivaldi nor Asgard."

"I vow," she said quickly.

"If you fail, Loki, all the treasures of the gods will be revoked. Every one. Ragnarok will receive you on your return."

Janessa felt that Ragnarok, the end of the world, was now, as she was herded with Loki to the entrance of the cavern. The light outside, here above, astonished her. Surely, it should be night, as dark here as it was inside the cavern and inside herself. This was all-time, where perhaps only a moment had passed since she so happily sailed to Asgard on the deck of the *Skidbladnir*. The last-known voyage of the great ship *Skidbladnir*, she thought.

With sunglasses on, two of the elves came aboveground with them, to see them off.

"What do you vow," she asked, "that the remaining treasures will not be revoked and those already taken will be returned?"

"This involves Loki, not you."

"This does not involve Loki," she said. "This involves an agreement between you and me."

There was murmuring among them, then a nodding of the two bespectacled heads. "As verification of our agreement, we will release the boar." Instantly, there was Golden-bristle, hovering, and the ground below illuminated in reverse shadow. The elves said, "What is your verification?"

She was tempted to call on the power of the ring, to see if they had returned it, too, so she may yet be saved by Odin, Freyr, Thor, Heimdall, Hoenir, one or all. Instead, she removed it, knowing the power of the ring was over and she could not wear it into her world anyway. She held the ring out to them solemnly, as though they understood this as an act of commitment and trust. The two nodded again and one of them took the ring. Her finger felt cold and bare.

"May I voice farewell to Freyr?" she asked, a demi-semiquaver in her voice.

"The golden boar will convey your farewell."

Once again they nodded, to her and then to Golden-bristle, as though giving permission for her to speak to the animal. She knew the boar already knew, but she moved close and, receiving no protest from the elves, reached up and stroked the gilded flank and made mental farewells. If she said them, she was afraid the words would yank on her tear ducts like a bell rope, and she had been acting so brave.

Since they'd been aboveground, Loki had said nothing, had simply been standing, holding the gold net which carried the coal that would guide their way. Now he transferred the silver handle to his mouth, drew his shoulders toward his ears, and stretched his arms until they feathered and became wings. Janessa wondered if Freya knew Loki had her falcon shape again.

"I will send the visors," she said. Clinging to feathers, ready for takeoff, she was unable to say good-bye, and did not want to be insincere and say thank you.

"Go with grace and take our valediction with you," they called out as the falcon rose. Valediction? What did that mean? They had given her nothing to take except herself, and though she was leaving here, she didn't know whether she would end up anywhere. Perhaps she had crossed too many time bands. Still, standing there below, waving, they did look just as silly in sunglasses as the gods did, though this didn't delight her. She wasn't delighted about anything—about leaving, the flight, being free, or going home or wherever she was going. She gripped the falcon's neck feathers, leaned her head between the powerful shoulders, and did not even look one last time for the Rainbow Bridge or the World Tree, or the Ice Mountains or the hole in the cloud. She didn't much care whether Loki found the way or not.

Had she fallen asleep? She jerked to awareness, realizing she had been riding a falcon, Loki. He had found his way, she saw, as he landed on the window ledge of her hospital room. Squawking in surprise at the two Janessas, the bird extended a wing and leaned to one side for her to slide off his back and into herself on the bed.

"Janessa!" he cried, looking at her helpless there. Then immediately he asked, "Where are sunglasses?"

Sunglasses. She had almost forgotten.

"There, in the bottom of the closet."

"Closet?"

Didn't they have closets in Asgard? "Open the door over there." She pointed, and he opened the door. "Do you see a bag?"

"Bag?"

"A pouch," she said. "Probably on the bottom."

When he picked it up and opened it, a look of glee came over his face. "It rattles," he said, shaking the bag, rumpling it with delight before he began perching sunglasses on his nose and ears.

She had the feeling she had just given Loki a collection of sunglasses. What did she care? What could she do about it if he didn't take them to the elves? Would the elves really revoke the gifts? Could they really start Ragnarok? They'd already had Ragnarok. Hadn't she seen Freyr's tomb?

"Which pair would you like?" she asked. Maybe giving him first choice would satisfy him. Maybe he would take the other pairs to the elves.

He left on a pair that was royal purple with rhinestones at the corners, and put the others in the bag. With the bag in his mouth, he leaped back to the windowsill and by the time he was there, he was the falcon again. Standing on the sill he shook wings, shook arms, wings, arms, being falcon, Loki, falcon, Loki, on and off like strobe lights.

"You are a brave one, Janessa," he said as Loki, his words muffled around the bag he held in his mouth. Then with one more shake of the wings he was gone—as quick as a falcon, as quick as never was.

Brave, huh, she thought, not impressed with his quicksilver magic, showing off his choices when she had no choice. Being a feather or a fish egg or following the command of the elves to move from the top step of the entrance to the cavern, or lying here with Crutchfield tongs. Or being thrown from a car. She had no choice. Dr. Gilder lied. He said she could make rules for her own life, but she couldn't. What choice did she have right now, except to be here, with the same fool lunch from all-time ago still on the tray? She stretched and held her hand over it. Warm. Incredible. She'd been gone no-time. Choices. Indeed. Here she was back in the hospital bed and the day of the cast was almost upon her. So much for choices.

She slapped the nurse-call button and when a nurse said, "May we help you, Janessa?" she replied in a militant, marching voice, "I want Dr. Gilder." On the digital clock above her, she timed him and he was there in two minutes, walking slowly for the first time ever, instead of attacking the room in his brisk bounce.

"Tell me," he said in a calm, quiet voice, heading straight for the bed, lifting a chair to bring with him.

When she opened her mouth to roar at him for all his lies about her choices, she said, "Arms. Daddy's arms." The words absolutely amazed her, but unplugged something that had been locked inside. Her mouth ran on. "He had arms with all this ruffly red-gold hair just like Daddy and when he was pushing me over, trying to push me out of the car and I was trying to hold on to him, the sun was shining in until all I saw was that arm, all full of copper-colored hair and when Daddy came the other night without his suit coat, I didn't want him here and I didn't know why I didn't want him here and I didn't know what was the matter with me because I love him and I felt like I hated him and it was his arms."

She didn't bellow or whimper but huge tears formed and plopped down the side of her face, following the track to the ears. Of all the things that had happened, that seemed the most incredibly sad thing, that she'd hated Daddy and was afraid of Daddy's arms.

"It's all right. It's good that you know what it is."

"But I don't want to see Daddy's arms. I don't ever want to see Daddy's arms. That makes me hate myself."

"No, no, look at those arms, that man's arms, in the car."

She didn't have to look. Her eyes were filled with short, wiry, red-gold hairs covering a freckled arm.

"Look at that arm and see that it isn't your father's arm. This arm, the one in the car, is trying to hurt you. Your father's arms are kind arms, loving arms."

Internally, she nodded. Those arms had swung her up and up, as they later swung Donna and Billy. Those arms held the bike when she was learning to ride. Those arms played wonderful cello music but that's where she was stuck, those bare arms moving back and forth across the cello as the man's arms had moved back and forth to shove her out of the car.

"Think about it, Janessa. Think about smashing into that pavement, think about it again and again until you realize it's not happening anymore. It's something that happened to you, him grabbing you, him taking you with him in the car, him pushing you out of the car. But it's not happening anymore. It's over. It's only in your mind, now. It can't keep hurting you. Look at the man. Look at his arms. Look at his face. Look in his eyes. He can't hurt you anymore."

"But he can," she said, "he can. They haven't caught him, have they?"

"No, they haven't, but I imagine he's far away from here. And even if he's not, there are lots of people looking for him and there will be lots of people watching out for you. Especially yourself."

"That's the truth," she said. She would never in her whole life open the door of a store without first looking in to see what was happening inside. She caught herself in the thought, the thought of being out there somewhere where she might open a door. She came out of the thought as out of a trance and saw that Dr. Gilder had idly taken the horizontal output tube out of his pocket and was holding it in his hand.

Suddenly she was tired of this stupid daily game. She pointed across the room and said, "You can put it on top of the television set."

He cocked his head, nodded, and complied.

It wasn't that she was ready to watch TV, but she wanted that tube out of his pocket. As he turned back toward her, she startled herself again when she said, "I want to go home."

The silence was deeper, thicker, stronger than ever it was in the caverns of Ivaldi while they were waiting for the one elf to return with Loki. Or yesterday morning, when she and Dr. Gilder sat at stalemate. For a moment, they both kept straight, impassive faces. Then, at just the same time, they brightened in surprise.

With emphasis and animation, she repeated the words. "I want to go home!" She grinned, then laughed. Then laughed and laughed and laughed, and said again and again, "I want to go home, I want to go home!"

Dr. Gilder laughed, hugged her and said, "You're wonderful, Janessa."

The next thing she said was, "I want to see Lynn." Never mind that she would be going home in a couple of days, whether she wanted to go or not. Getting the cast meant going home. She would see Lynn then, as much as she wanted, but she wanted to see Lynn now, today. She wanted, actually, to see everyone, Billy and Donna and her other friends, but most of all Lynn. She would start with Lynn. "Will you please hand me the phone so I can call my parents?"

When he handed her the phone, she set it on her chest where such things as telephones and checkerboards were set. And she called her father, since he was always either there or someone knew where he was, whereas at Mother's office she was just as apt to get the answering machine as Mother.

"Hi, Daddy, it's Messa," she said.

When he said, "Ba-aby!" his voice dove through the telephone and she didn't feel babyish at all.

"Daddy, I want you to go get Lynn and bring her to see

me." There was a moment of silence. Was he alarmed? Pleased? "Right now, if you can."

There was another silence before he said, "Of course."

"Mom, too," she said.

And he said, "Of course."

When Dr. Gilder took back the phone, she said, "I guess I should have said after school."

"Why?" he asked.

"Well, maybe she'll think I'm dying, or something. Maybe she'll be scared."

Dr. Gilder grinned. "She'll find out soon enough."

"Now I guess Daddy will have to call her parents for permission. I've caused lots of trouble."

"No one will mind," Dr. Gilder said. "You deserve it."

"Do I?" she asked. Something about the idea of deserving pleased her deeply.

Out of habit, almost, she pulled the worktable toward her and slid a sheet of origami paper onto her fingers and began folding a boat. She forgot that Dr. Gilder was there, and she wanted to summon Freyr and let him know she was all right.

As she was finishing the boat, pulling out the sails, Dr. Gilder said, "I like that a lot, Janessa. Will you teach me to make one?" and before she knew what he was doing, he took it from her and began dismantling the ship.

She shrieked, "No-o-o-o," but he had already trimmed the sail, lowered the mast and unfolded the sides. With a gasp, she looked out the window but no prow of *Skid-*

bladnir was melding through. All she saw was a windowful of sky. And beyond it, only sky.

"I didn't mean to be rude," he said, handing back the creased paper. "Did you?" He flipped his fingers and hands as though tossing them to the air. "You have impressed me with this origami. I only wanted to learn how to do one."

Her breath was locked inside her chest and she could not release any of it for a moment, but when no *Skidbladnir* appeared, she said, "It's okay. I'm sorry." And she showed him how to fold a paper boat.

After Dr. Gilder left, she lay there happily, waiting. Happy. She could scarcely remember the time before being grabbed from the store, the time when she was happy. But she was happy now and it felt good. Familiar.

Wanting to share this goodness with someone right now, without having to wait for Dad and Mother and Lynn, she reached for another origami paper and, carefully, almost reverently, folded a boat. Of course Freyr had not come, because it was Dr. Gilder who'd unfolded the boat. When she had finished the boat she folded another and another and another until the bed was as full of boats as it had once been full of rabbits. But she never unfolded one. She had made her last voyage on the *Skidbladnir*.

Then here came Daddy, almost timidly, face full of worry, and alone.

"Where's Lynn?" she asked.

"In the hall," he said, nodding, only half smiling. "In

the hall with Mother. I wanted to check on you first. Are you okay?"

"Oh," she said, understanding. They must have all been scared. "I'm fine, Daddy. I'm really fine. I'm your Messa."

There was a puzzled, strained, wondering look on his face as he came to hug her. "Baby, oh, baby," he said, leaning close, touching her head, her shoulders, doing the most he could for a hug.

"I want you to take off your coat," she said.

Without questioning, he had that coat off.

"Roll up your sleeves," she said.

And with the scrunched, puzzled face, he rolled.

"I need a red-gold, hairy-armed, bare-armed hug," she said, and his tight face melted into a red-gold smile and he hugged her and hugged her and she felt cello music in those arms.

"Daddy, Daddy, Daddy, Daddy, Daddy," she said, but she didn't cry. With a start, she realized she didn't remember music in Asgard, no music at all, no music such as her father played for her, no life music. Surely, surely they had music, she thought. Did she simply not remember, or did she not hear it because she was out of her time?

When Dad let go of her he stepped to the door and motioned into the hall and here came Lynn, moving slowly, shyly, as though they didn't really know each other anymore. Mother came behind, hand on Lynn's shoulder for encouragement. Lynn looked at Janessa, then glanced at the apparatus, the traction, the Crutchfield tongs, and winced in pain.

The look on Lynn's face pinched Janessa's tear ducts and Janessa started crying, tears splashing up and out in spatters. Unsure, Lynn stepped back and Mother closed arms around her. Janessa cried for all the weeks of cards and notes Lynn had sent with no response, and for everything else for all these weeks. She cried just as loud and hard as she ever had at her parents coming and going those first days. Enough tears to float the ark. Enough to float the *Skidbladnir*.

All at once, all the tears seemed utterly ridiculous. She felt wonderful and some of her best people were here in this room and she laughed in the middle of the crying, laughed more and nearly choked herself with laughing. Mother laughed and Dad laughed and finally Lynn laughed, until they had layers of laughter sailing around the room like windblown origami papers—red, rose, turquoise, and royal blue laughter.

ABOUT THE AUTHOR

Doris Buchanan Smith has written many books for young readers, including *Return to Bitter Creek*, *Last Was Lloyd*, *The First Hard Times*, *Laura Upside-Down*, and *Tough Chauncey*.

Of *Voyages*, she says: "All of my books have begun with a character wandering around in my head, but *Voyages* began with a magical ship from Norse mythology. Along the way, there were many adventures of the imagination and—for myself, as well as for my character, Janessa— the voyage was both difficult and dazzling."

The mother of five grown children, Ms. Smith grew up in Atlanta and now lives in Brunswick, Georgia. During the summer, she retreats to a rustic cabin in Hayesville, North Carolina.